Harlequin Romance®
presents
an exciting new duet by
international bestselling author

LUCY GORDON

Where there's a will, there's a wedding!

Rinaldo and Gino Farnese are wealthy,
proud, passionate brothers who live in the
heart of Tuscany, Italy. Their late father's will brings
one surprise that ultimately leads to two more—
a bride for each of them!

Book 1: *Rinaldo's Inherited Bride*, #3799

And don't miss book 2:
Gino's Arranged Bride, #3807
On sale August 2004

Dear Reader,

When two brothers love the same woman, the result is a mighty clash in the fierce heat of Tuscany, a place where the colors are darker, and the air crackles with danger.

Rinaldo and Gino share a powerful love of the land, and have the same emotional, virile intensity. But fate has turned Rinaldo into a gruff, hard-bitten cynic, while Gino, his younger brother, likes to laugh and still has traces of the boy in his carefree nature.

Their peace is wrecked by Alex, from England, who has unexpectedly inherited a claim to some of their farm. Then no amount of brotherly love can count against the passion for a woman both see as an interloper, yet whom neither can resist.

Elegant, determined, a success in her high-powered career, Alex is sure she can deal with the Farnese brothers. She doesn't know that they have tossed a coin for her, nor would she care. She will choose the man she wants.

One will win the prize. The other will be cast out to find his destiny among strangers.

Best wishes,

Lucy Gordon

RINALDO'S INHERITED BRIDE

Lucy Gordon

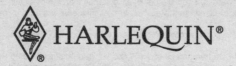

TORONTO • NEW YORK • LONDON
AMSTERDAM • PARIS • SYDNEY • HAMBURG
STOCKHOLM • ATHENS • TOKYO • MILAN • MADRID
PRAGUE • WARSAW • BUDAPEST • AUCKLAND

ISBN 0-373-03799-6

RINALDO'S INHERITED BRIDE

First North American Publication 2004.

Copyright © 2004 by Lucy Gordon.

CHAPTER ONE

'HE HATES me. He really hates me!'

Alex had expected some resentment, but not this bleak hostility. All the way out from England to Italy she had wondered about Rinaldo and Gino Farnese, the two men she had partly dispossessed.

Now, meeting Rinaldo's eyes across his father's grave, she thought she had never seen so much concentrated bitterness in one human being.

She blinked, thinking it might be an illusion of the brilliant Italian sun. Here there were sharp edges like sword blades, and dark shadows that swallowed light; hot colours, red, orange, deep yellow, black. Vibrant. Intense. Dangerous.

Now I'm getting fanciful, she thought.

But the danger was there, in the fury-filled eyes of Rinaldo Farnese, still watching her.

Isidoro, her elderly Italian lawyer, had pointed out the two Farnese brothers, but even without that she would have known them. The family likeness was clear. Both men were tall, with lean, fine-featured faces and dark, brilliant eyes.

Gino, clearly the younger, looked as though he had a softer side. There was a touch of curl in his hair, and a curve to his mouth that suggested humour, flirtation, delight.

But there was nothing soft about Rinaldo. His face might have been carved from granite. He seemed to be in his late thirties, with a high forehead and a nose that only just escaped being hooked. It was the most powerful feature in a powerful face.

Even at this distance Alex could detect a tension so fierce that it threatened to tear him apart. He was holding it back with a supreme effort. His grim, taut mouth revealed that, and the set of his chin.

There would be no yielding from him, Alex thought. No relenting. No forgiveness.

But why should she think she needed forgiveness from Rinaldo Farnese? She'd done him no wrong.

But he had been wronged, not by her, but by the father who had mortgaged a third of the family property, and left his sons to find out, brutally, after his death.

'Vincente Farnese was a delightful fellow,' Isidoro had told her. 'But he had this terrible habit of putting off awkward moments and hoping for a miracle. Rinaldo took charge as much as possible, but the old boy still left him a nasty surprise at the end. Can't blame him for being a bit put out.'

But the man facing her over the grave wasn't 'a bit put out.' He was ready to do murder.

'I guess I shouldn't have come to their father's funeral,' she murmured to Isidoro.

'No, they probably think you're gloating.'

'I just wanted to meet them, reassure them that I'll give them a fair chance to redeem the mortgage.'

'Alex, haven't you understood? As far as these men are concerned they owe you nothing, and you're a usurper. Offering a "fair chance" to pay you is a recipe for bloodshed. Let's get out of here fast.'

'You go. I'm not running away from them.'

'You may wish you had,' he said gloomily.

'Nonsense, what can they do to me?'

It had seemed so easy a week ago, sitting in the elegant London restaurant with David.

'This inheritance will probably pay for your partnership,' he'd observed.

'And a lot of other things too,' she said, smiling, and thinking of the dream home that they would share after their wedding.

David didn't answer this directly, but he raised his champagne glass in salute.

David Edwards was part of Alex's life plan. At forty, neatly handsome in a pin-striped kind of way, he was the head of a firm of very expensive, very prestigious London accountants.

Alex had started work for them eight years ago, after passing her accountancy exams with top honours. She had always known that one day she would be a partner, just as one day she would marry David.

Eight years had transformed her from a rather shy, awkward girl, more at home with figures than people, into a stunning, sophisticated woman.

It was David himself who had unknowingly started the transformation in her early days with the firm. Struck by his looks, she had longed to attract his attention.

After six months, without success, she had overheard him casually asking a colleague, 'Who's the pudding in the red dress?'

He had passed on, unaware that the 'pudding' had heard him and was choking back misery and anger.

Two days later David announced his engagement to the daughter of the senior partner.

Alex had plunged into her work. For the next five years she allowed herself only the most passing relationships. At the end of that time her long hours and excellent results had made her a power in the firm.

By then the senior partner had retired and David had taken over the position. Now he no longer needed his father-in-law's influence, although it was only ill-natured people who openly made a connection between that and his divorce.

Alex had worked as hard on transforming herself as she had on her job. Her body represented the triumph of the workout. Her legs were long and slender enough to risk the shortest skirts. The tightest of dresses found no extra pounds on her.

Her fair hair was short, expertly cut and shaped, nestling close to her neat head on top of a long, elegant neck. She was a highly finished work of art, her mind as perfectly ordered as her appearance.

She and David became an item, and everyone knew that soon the firm's two stars would link up and run the place together.

Now it seemed that nothing could be better structured. Her inheritance would be followed by her partnership, and then by her marriage.

'Of course it might take a little time to arrange,' David mused now. 'You haven't actually inherited part of the property, have you?'

'No, just the money that was loaned against it. Enrico assigned the debt to me in his will. So the Farnese brothers owe me a large sum of money, and if they can't repay in a reasonable time, that's when I can claim some of the actual farm.'

'Either that or sell your interest to someone else, which would make more sense. What would you want with one third of a farm?'

'Nothing, but I'd feel uneasy about doing that. I have to give the Farneses every chance to pay me first.'

'Sure, and, as I said, it may take time. So don't rush back. Take as long as you need and do it properly.'

Alex smiled, thinking fondly how understanding he was. It would make everything easier.

'You haven't seen much of your Italian relatives, have you?' David asked now.

'My mother was Enrico Mori's niece. He came to visit us a couple of times. He was an excitable man, very intense and emotional. Just like her.'

'But not like you?'

She laughed. 'Well, I couldn't afford to be intense and emotional. Mum filled the house with her melodrama. I adored her, but I suppose I developed my common sense as a reaction. One of us had to be cool, calm and collected.

'I remember Enrico frowning and saying, ''You must be like your English Poppa,'' and it wasn't a compliment. Poppa died when I was twelve, but I remember he never shouted or lost his temper.'

'And you don't either.'

'What's the point? It's better to talk things out sensibly. Mum used to say that one day we'd visit Italy together, and I'd ''see the light''. She even raised me to speak Italian and some Tuscan dialect, so that I wouldn't be all at sea when we visited ''my other country''.'

'But you never went?'

'She became ill. When she died three years ago Enrico came over and I met him again.'

'Are you his only heir?'

'No, there are some distant cousins who inherit his house and land. He was a rich man, with no wife or children. He lived alone in Florence, having a great old time, drinking and chasing women.'

'So where did Vincente Farnese come into this?'

'They were old friends. A few years ago he borrowed some money from Enrico, and charged it against Belluna, that's the farm. Last week, apparently, they went out on a binge, drove the car home, and had the accident that killed them both.'

'And his sons had no idea that there was a hefty mortgage against the land?'

'Not until Enrico's will was read, apparently.'

'So you're going right into the lion's den? Be careful.'

'You surely don't think I'll be assassinated down a dark lane? I shall go to Florence, make an arrangement with the Farnese brothers, and then come home.'

'And if they can't raise the money, and you sell your interest to an outsider? Will they sit quiet for that?'

'Don't be melodramatic, David,' she said, laughing. 'I'm sure they're reasonable people, just as I am. We'll sort it all out, somehow.'

'Reasonable?' Rinaldo snapped. 'Our father charged a huge loan against this property without telling us, and the lawyers want us to be reasonable?'

Gino sighed. 'I still can't take it in,' he said. 'How could Poppa have kept such a secret for so long, especially from you?'

The light was fading, for the evening was well advanced. Standing by the window of his home, looking out over the hills and fields that stretched into the distance, earth that he had cultivated with his own hands, sometimes at terrible cost, Rinaldo knew that he must cling onto this, or go mad.

'You and I are Poppa's heirs and the legal owners of Belluna,' Gino pointed out. 'This woman can't change that.'

'She can if we can't pay up. If she doesn't get her cash

she can claim one third of Belluna. Poppa never made any repayments, so now we owe the whole amount, plus interest.'

'Well, I suppose we gained from having all that money,' Gino mused.

'That's true,' Rinaldo admitted reluctantly. 'It paid for the new machinery, the hire of extra labourers, the best fertiliser, which has greatly improved our crops. All that cost a fortune. Poppa just said he'd won the lottery.'

'And we believed it until the wills were read,' Gino said heavily. 'That's what hurts, that he left us to find out like that.' But then he gave a heavy sigh. 'Still, I suppose we shouldn't blame him. He didn't know he was going to die suddenly. Do we know anything about this woman, apart from the fact that she's English?'

'According to the lawyer her name is Alexandra Dacre. She's in her late twenties, an accountant, and lives in London.'

'I don't like the sound of her,' Gino sighed.

'Neither do I. This is a cold-blooded Anglo-Saxon. She works with money, and that's all she'll care about.'

He raised his head suddenly, and there was a fierce intensity in his eyes.

'We have no choice,' he said. *'We have to get rid of her.'*

Gino jumped. *'How? Rinaldo, for pity's sake—!'*

At that moment he could have believed his brother capable of any cruel act.

Rinaldo gave a brief smile, which had the strange effect of making his face even more grim than before.

'Calm down,' he said. 'I'm not planning murder. I don't say the idea isn't appealing, but it's not what I meant. I want to dispose of her legally.'

'So we have to pay her.'

'How? All the money we have is ploughed into the land until harvest. We're already overdrawn at the bank, and a loan would be at a ruinous rate of interest.'

'Can't our lawyer suggest something?'

'He's going soft in the head. Since she's single he had the brilliant idea that one of us marry her.'

'That's it!' Gino cried. 'The perfect answer. All problems solved.'

He spread his hands in a triumphant gesture and gave his attractive, easy laugh. He was twenty-seven and there was still a touch of the boy about him.

'So now we have to meet her,' he said. 'I wonder if she'll come to Poppa's funeral?'

'She won't dare!' Rinaldo snapped. 'Now, come and have supper. Teresa's been getting it ready.'

In the kitchen they found Teresa, the elderly housekeeper, laying the table. As she worked she wept. It had been like that every day since Vincente had died.

Rinaldo wasn't hungry, but he knew that to say so would be to upset the old woman even more. Instead he placed a gentle hand on her shoulder, silently comforting her until she stopped weeping.

'That's better now,' he said kindly. 'You know how Poppa hated long faces.'

She nodded. 'Always laughing,' she said huskily. 'Even if the crops failed, he would find something to laugh at. He was a rare one.'

'Yes, he was,' Rinaldo agreed. 'And we must remember him like that.'

She looked at the chair by the great kitchen range, where Vincente had often sat.

'He should be there,' she said. 'Telling funny stories, making silly jokes. Do you remember how terrible his jokes were?'

Rinaldo nodded. 'And the worst puns I ever heard.'

Gino came in and gave Teresa a big, generous hug. He was a young man who hugged people easily, and it made him loved wherever he went. Now it was enough to start her crying again, and he held her patiently in his strong arms until she was ready to stop.

Rinaldo left them and went outside. When he'd gone Teresa muttered, 'He's lost so many of those he loved, and each time I've seen his face grow a little darker, a little more bleak.'

Gino nodded. He knew Teresa was talking about Rinaldo's wife Maria, and their baby son, both dead in the second year of their marriage.

'If they'd lived, the little boy would have been nearly ten by now,' he reflected. 'And they'd probably have had several more children. This house would have been full of kids. I'd have had nephews and nieces to teach mischief to, instead of—'

He looked up at the building that was much too large for the three people who shared it.

'Now he only has you,' Teresa agreed.

'And you. And that daft mutt. Sometimes I think Brutus means more to him than any other creature, because he was Maria's dog. Apart from that he loves the farm, and he's possessive about it because he has so little else. I hope Signorina Dacre has a lot of nerve, because she's going to need it.'

Rinaldo returned with the large indeterminate animal Gino had stigmatised as 'that daft mutt'. Brutus had an air of amiability mixed with anarchy, plus huge feet. Ignoring Teresa's look of disapproval he parked himself under the table, close to his master.

Over pasta and mushrooms Gino said, lightly, 'So I suppose one of us has to marry the English woman.'

'When you say "one of us" you mean me, I suppose,' Rinaldo growled. 'You wouldn't like settling down with a wife, not if it meant having to stop your nonsense. Besides, she evidently has an orderly mind, which means she'd be driven nuts by you in five minutes.'

'Then you should be the one,' Gino said.

'No, thank you.' Rinaldo's tone was a warning.

'But you're the head of the family now. I think it's your duty. Hey—what are you doing with that wine?'

'Preparing to pour it over your head if you don't shut up.'

'But we have to do something. We need a master plan.'

His brother replaced the wine on the table, annoyance giving way to faint amusement. Gino's flippancy might often be annoying, but it was served up with a generous helping of charm.

Rinaldo would have declared himself immune to that charm. Even so, he regarded his brother with a wry look that was almost a grin.

'Then get to work,' he said. 'Make her head spin.'

'I've got a better idea. Let's toss for her.'

'For pity's sake grow up!'

'Seriously, let Fate make the decision.'

'If I go through with this charade, I don't want to hear it mentioned again. Hurry up and get it over with!'

Gino took a coin from his pocket and flipped it high in the air. 'Call!'

'Tails.'

Gino caught the coin and slapped it down on the back of his hand.

'Tails!' he said. 'She's all yours.'

Rinaldo groaned. 'I thought you were using your two-headed coin or I wouldn't have played.'

'As if I'd do a thing like that!' Gino sounded aggrieved.

'I've known times when—well, never mind. I'm not interested. You can have her.'

He rose and drained his glass before Gino could answer. He didn't feel that he could stand much more of this conversation.

Gino went to bed first. He was young. Even in his grief for a beloved father he slept easily.

Rinaldo could barely remember what it was to sleep peacefully. When the house was quiet he slipped out. The moon was up, casting a livid white glow over the earth. The light was neither soft nor alluring, but harsh, showing him outlines of trees and hills in brutal relief.

That was the land to which he'd given his whole life. Here, in this soft earth, he'd lain one night with a girl who smelled of flowers and joy, whispering words of love.

'Soon it will be our wedding day, love of my life—come to me—be mine always.'

And she had come to him in passion and tenderness, generous and giving, nothing held back, her body young and pliable in his arms.

But for such a little time.

One year and six months from the date of their wedding to the day he'd buried his wife and child together.

And his heart with them.

He walked on. He could have trodden this journey with his eyes closed. Every inch of this land was part of his being. He knew its moods, how it could be harsh, brutal, sometimes generous with its bounty but more often demanding a cruel price.

Until today he had paid the price, not always willingly, sometimes in anguish and bitterness, but he had paid it.

And now this.

He lost track of time, seeing nothing with his outer eye. What he could see, inwardly, was Vincente, roaring with laughter as he tossed his baby son, Gino, up into the air, then turned to smile lovingly on the child Rinaldo.

'Remember when I used to do that with you, my son? Now we are men together.'

And his own eager response. 'Yes, Poppa!'

He had been eight years old, and his father had known by instinct what to say to drive out jealousy of the new baby, and make him happy.

Poppa, who had believed that the world was a good place because there was always warmth and love and generosity, and who had tried to make him believe it too.

Poppa, his ally in a hundred childhood pranks. 'We won't tell Mamma, it would only worry her.'

But these images were succeeded by another, one he hadn't seen, but which he now realised had been there all along: the old man, round faced and white whiskered, laughing up his sleeve at the little joke he'd played on his sons, and particularly on his forceful elder son.

Vincente hadn't seen the danger. So there had been no warning, no chance to be prepared. Rinaldo had always loved his father, but at this moment it was hard not to hate him.

The darkness was turning to the first grey of dawn. He had walked for miles, and now it was time to walk back and make ready for the biggest fight of his life.

CHAPTER TWO

RINALDO FARNESE finally dragged his eyes away from the woman who was his enemy. He had noted dispassionately that she was beautiful in a glossy, city-bred kind of way that would have increased his hostility if it hadn't been at fever pitch already. Everything about her confirmed his suspicions, from her fair hair to her elegant clothes.

It was time for the mourners to speak over the grave. There were many, for Vincente had been popular. Some were elderly men, 'partners in crime' who had spent days in the sun with him, drinking wine and remembering the old times.

There were several middle-aged and elderly women, hinting wistfully at sweet memories, under the jealous eyes of their menfolk.

Finally there were his sons. Gino spoke movingly, recalling his father's gentleness and sweet temper, his ready laughter.

'He'd had a hard life,' he recalled, 'working very long hours, every day for years, so that his family might prosper. But it never soured him, and to the end of his life, nothing delighted him as much as a practical joke.'

Then he fell silent, and a soft ripple ran around the crowd. By now all of them knew about Vincente's last practical joke.

A heaviness seemed to come over Gino as he realised what he had said. The light went out of his attractive young face, and his eyes sought his brother with a touch of desperation.

Rinaldo's face revealed nothing. With a brief nod at Gino he stepped up to take his place.

'My father was a man who could win love,' he said, speaking almost curtly. 'That much is proved by the presence of so many of his friends today. It is no more than he deserved. I thank each of you for coming to do him honour.'

That was all. The words were jerked from him as if by force. His face might have been made of stone.

The mourners began to drift away from the grave. Rinaldo gave Alex a last look and turned, touching Gino's arm to indicate for him to come too.

'Wait,' Gino said.

'No,' Rinaldo was following his gaze.

'We've got to meet her some time. Besides—' he gave a soft whistle. 'She's beautiful.'

'Remember where you are and show respect,' Rinaldo said quietly.

'Poppa wouldn't mind. He'd have been the first to whistle. Rinaldo, have you ever seen such a beauty?'

'I'm happy for you,' his brother said without looking at him. 'Your job should be easier.'

Gino had caught the lawyer's eye and raised his eyebrows, inclining his head slightly in Alex's direction. Isidoro nodded and Gino began to make his way across to them.

Alex caught the look they exchanged, then she focused on Gino. An engaging young man, she thought. Even dressed in black, he had a kind of brightness about him. His handsome face was fresh, eager, open.

It had little to do with his youth. It was more a natural

joyousness in his nature that would be with him all his life, unless something happened to sour it.

'Gino, this is Signorina Alexandra Dacre,' Isidoro hastened to make the introductions. 'Enrico was her great-uncle.'

'Yes, I've heard of Signorina Dacre.' Gino's smile had an almost conspiratorial quality, as if to suggest that they were all in this mess together.

'I'm beginning to feel as if the whole of Florence has heard of me,' she said, smiling back and beginning to like him.

'The whole of Tuscany,' he said. 'Sensations like this don't happen every day.'

'I gather you knew nothing about it,' Alex said.

'Nothing at all, until the lawyers were going through the paperwork.'

'What a nasty shock. I'm surprised you want to shake my hand.'

'It isn't your fault,' Gino said at once.

His grasp, like everything about him, was warm, enclosing her hand in both of his.

'We must meet properly and talk,' he said.

'Yes, there's a lot to talk about,' she agreed. Suddenly she burst out, 'Did I do wrong to come to your father's funeral? Perhaps it was tasteless of me, but I only—look, I meant well.'

'Yes, it was tasteless of you,' said a dry, ironic voice. 'You have no place here. Why did you come?'

'Rinaldo, please,' Gino said in a swift, soft voice.

'No, he's right,' Alex said hastily. 'I made a mistake. I'll go now.'

'But we're having a reception in the Hotel Favello,' Gino said. 'Enrico was Poppa's dearest friend, and you're part of Enrico's family, so naturally you're invited.'

He glanced at his brother, waiting for his confirmation. For a moment Rinaldo's manners warred with his hostility. At last he shrugged and said briefly, 'Of course.'

He turned away without waiting for her answer.

'The hotel isn't far,' Gino said. 'I'll show you.'

'No need, I'm staying there,' Alex told him. 'I arrived last night.'

'Then shall we go?' He offered her his arm.

'Thank you, but I'll make my own way. You have guests who'll want your attention.'

She hurried away before he could argue, and rejoined Isidoro, who fell into step beside her.

'If you're going into the lion's den I'm coming with you,' he said.

'That might be a good idea after all,' she agreed.

As they walked the short distance to the hotel Alex said, 'He really did have a lot of friends, didn't he?'

'Yes, he was a much-loved man. But the people at the wake won't just be his friends and lovers. They'll be the vultures hovering over that mortgage, and you'll be very interesting to them.

'Watch out for a man called Montelli. He's greedy and unscrupulous, and if Rinaldo sees you talking to him it'll make him mad.'

'Well,' Alex said, apparently considering this, 'since everything I do is going to make that man angry, I think I'll just go right ahead and do what suits me.'

The Hotel Favello was a Renaissance building that had once belonged to the Favello family, wealthy and influential for centuries, now fallen on hard times.

It had been turned into a luxury hotel in such a way that every modern comfort was provided, but so discreetly that nothing seemed to have changed for centuries.

Alex went up to her room first, so as not to arrive too soon, wishing she had time for a shower. It was June and Florence was hotter than anything she had experienced in England. Standing in the sun, she had felt the heat spreading over her skin beneath her clothes, making her intensely aware of every inch of her body.

But there was no time for a shower if she were to join the reception. She mopped her brow and checked her appearance in the mirror. She looked, as always, immaculate.

It would have been over-the-top to wear black for a man she hadn't known, but she was formally dressed in a navy blue linen dress, with a matching coat, adorned only by one silver brooch. Now she tossed aside the coat before going downstairs.

She was relieved to see that the reception room was already crowded, so that she attracted little attention.

Isidoro scuttled to greet her and pointed out some of the others.

'The ones glowering at you in the corner are the other members of Enrico's family,' he said.

'Don't tell me they're annoyed with me too?' she exclaimed.

'Of course. They were expecting to inherit more.'

'So I'm in the firing line from both sides,' she said with a touch of exasperation. 'Oh, heavens!'

'This is Italy,' Isidoro said wryly. 'The home of the blood feud. Here they come.'

Two men and two women appeared solidly before Alex. Greetings were exchanged, not overtly hostile, but cautious. The older man, who seemed to be the spokesman for the group, muttered something about having 'necessary discussions' later.

Alex nodded agreement, and the group moved off. But

behind them was a middle-aged man of large proportions and an oily manner. He introduced himself as Leo Montelli, and said that the sooner they talked the better.

After him came another local landowner, and after him came the representative of a bank. Alex began to feel dizzy. One thing was clear. The message about who she was and why she was here had gone out loud and clear to everyone in the room.

It had certainly reached Rinaldo Farnese, who was watching her steadily. His face was inscrutable, but Alex had the feeling that he was mentally taking notes.

'Isidoro, I'm leaving,' she said. 'This shouldn't be happening here. It isn't seemly.'

'Shall I fix appointments with them for you?'

'Not yet,' she said quickly. 'I must talk to the Farneses first. For now I'll just slip away.'

'Look,' Isidoro said.

Rinaldo was cutting his way through the crowd until he reached her and said very softly, 'I want you to leave, right now. Your behaviour is unseemly.'

'Hey, now look—'

'How dare you dance on my father's grave! Leave right this moment or I'll put you out myself.'

'*Signore*—' Isidoro was vainly trying to claim his attention.

'I was about to leave anyway,' Alex said.

'To be sure, *signorina*, I believe you.'

'You'd better,' she said losing her temper. 'Signor Farnese, I dislike you at least as much as you dislike me, and I won't stand for being called a liar. If this wasn't a solemn occasion I would take the greatest pleasure in losing my temper in a way you wouldn't forget.'

She stormed out without giving him the chance to answer. If she could have sold the entire farm out from under him she would have done so at that moment.

The Hotel Favello was in the Piazza della Republica, in the medieval heart of Florence. Here Alex was close to the great buildings, the Palazzo Vecchio, the Duomo, whose huge bulk dominated the Florence skyline, the fascinating Ponte Vecchio over the River Arno, and many other places she had promised herself that she would visit before she left.

On the evening of the funeral she decided to eat out, preferably in a restaurant where she could gain a floodlit view of the buildings.

She'd had a shower as soon as she left the reception, but before getting dressed she had another one under cold water. Thankfully the onset of evening was making temperatures fall, and the room had good air-conditioning, but she felt as though the heat had penetrated down to the core of her.

She started to put on a pair of tights, but discarded them almost at once, disliking the suffocating sensation of anything clinging to her flesh. She rejected a bra for the same reason.

When she finally slipped on a white silk dress she wore only a slip and brief panties beneath, because that was the only way she felt her body could breathe.

Just as she was about to leave there was a knock on her door.

She opened it to find Rinaldo Farnese standing there.

He had removed the jacket of his smart black suit, and was holding it hooked over the shoulder of his white shirt, which had been pulled open at the throat. His hair was untidy, his face weary, and he looked as though he had discarded the strait-laced persona of the funeral with as much relief as she had discarded her coat.

'This won't take long,' he said, pushing the door further open and walking into the room.

'Hey, I didn't invite you in,' she protested.

'I didn't invite you either, but here you are,' he responded.

'And I'm just going out to dinner,' she said.

At this point a gentleman would have at least offered her a drink. Rinaldo's only response was a shrug.

'Then I'll be brief,' he said.

'Please do,' she replied crisply.

'First, I suppose I owe you an apology for my behaviour this afternoon.'

She gaped at him, totally taken aback. The last thing she had expected from this man was an apology.

'After you left I spoke to Isidoro who confirmed that you'd been about to depart of your own accord, and that you too had used the word unseemly.' He took a deep breath and spoke as though the words were jerked from him. 'I apologise for doubting your truthfulness.'

'I appreciate that,' she said, 'all the more because it half killed you to say it.'

'I'm not known for my social skills,' he agreed wryly.

'I'd never have guessed.'

'You think to disconcert me with irony? Don't bother.'

She nodded.

'You're right. You don't care enough about other people's opinions to mind whether you have social skills or not,' she said gravely. 'I'm sure rudeness has its advantages, besides being less trouble.'

This time there was no doubt that she got to him. He eyed her narrowly. Alex looked straight back at him.

'May I remind you that I only came to that reception

on your brother's invitation?' she said. 'It wasn't my idea, and I certainly wouldn't have come if I'd known what would happen. Perhaps it's I who owe you an apology for my clumsiness.'

They regarded each other warily, neither of them in the least mollified by the other's conciliatory words.

Despite her exasperation Alex was curious about him. After the sleek, smooth men she knew in London, meeting Rinaldo was like encountering a wild animal. The feelings that drove him were so powerful that she could almost feel them radiating from him. He was controlling them, but only just.

She thought of David, who never did anything that hadn't been planned beforehand. She couldn't imagine him losing control, but with Rinaldo Farnese she could imagine it only too easily.

Strangely the thought did not alarm her, but only increased her curiosity.

He began to stride impatiently about the room in a way that told her he was happier outdoors, and rooms suffocated him. Now she appreciated how tall he was, over six foot, broad-shouldered but lean. He was lithe, not graceful like his brother, but athletic, like a tightly coiled spring.

'So now you've seen them all,' he said. 'All the vultures who are lining up to swoop. They've calculated that your only interest is money. Are they wrong?'

'I—well, you're certainly direct.'

'I came here to know what your plans are. Is that direct enough for you?'

'My plans are fluid at the moment. I'm waiting to see what develops.'

'Do you fancy yourself as a farmer?'

'No, I'm not a farmer, nor do I have any ambitions to be one.'

'That is a wise decision. You would find us two to one against you.'

She surveyed him with her head a little on one side. 'You don't believe in sugar coating it, do you?'

'No,' he said simply, 'there's no point. What are your plans?'

'To discuss the situation with you. The vultures can think what they like. You get the first chance to redeem the loan. Look, I'm not a monster. I know money can be difficult. In my own country I'm an accountant—'

'I know,' he said impatiently. 'Somebody who works with money. And that's all you care about—money.'

'Enough!' she said in a sudden hard voice. 'I won't let you speak to me like that, I'm not responsible for this situation.'

'But you don't mind benefiting from it?'

'I don't mind benefiting under Enrico's will because that's what he wanted. I dare say he would have left me money, but his cash was tied up in you. You're acting as though I have no right to recover it. I'm sorry if it's come as a shock to you, but it isn't my fault that your father didn't tell you.'

'Be silent!' The words were swift and hostile and the look he turned on her was like a dagger. 'Do not speak of my father.'

'All right, but don't blame me for a situation I didn't create.'

He was silent for a moment and she could see that she had taken him aback. After a while he said, 'Nobody doubts your right to accept your inheritance, but I suggest that you be careful how you go about it.'

'What you mean is that you *demand* that I go about it in the way that suits you,' she replied at once.

Something that might almost have been a smile passed over his bleak face and was gone.

'Let us say that you should consider the whole complex situation before you rush to a decision,' he said at last. 'Every penny the farm has is tied up until the harvest. You'll get your money, but in instalments.'

'That's no use to me. I have my own plans.'

He regarded her. 'If your plans conflict with mine, let me advise you to drop them. In the meantime, you should leave Italy.'

'No,' she said bluntly.

'I strongly advise you—'

'The answer is no.'

'*Signorina*,' Rinaldo said softly, 'you do not know this country.'

'All the more reason for remaining. I'm part Italian and this is my country too.'

'You misunderstand. When I said "this country" I didn't mean Italy. I meant Tuscany. You're not in cool, civilised England now. This is a dangerous place for intruders. Those dark hills look inviting, but too often they've hidden brigands who recognised no law but their own.'

'And I'll bet they were led by someone just like you,' she challenged him back. 'Someone who thought he had only to speak and the world trembled. Do you see me trembling?'

'Perhaps you would be wiser if you did.'

'Stop trying to scare me. It won't work. I'll do what suits me, *when* it suits me. If you don't like it—tough. After all, that's the code you live by yourself.'

This was a shot in the dark. She barely knew him, but

instinct would have told her the sort of man he was, even if his own words and attitude hadn't made it pretty plain. He was overbearing, and he wouldn't be too scrupulous about how he got his own way. That was her estimation of him.

The sooner he realised that, in her, he'd met his match, the better.

'Are you suggesting that I'm a brigand, *signorina*?'

'I think you could be if you felt it necessary.'

'And *will* it be necessary?'

'You tell me. I imagine we judge the matter differently. I don't want instalments. I need a lump sum, fairly soon. I have a once-in-a-lifetime chance, and to seize it I need money. But we can work it out. Perhaps someone else can take over the mortgage—a bank or something.'

Suddenly his face was dark, distorted.

'Don't try to involve strangers in this,' he said fiercely. 'Do you think I'd allow them to come interfering—dictating—*Maria vergine*!'

He slammed one hand into the other.

'I've had enough of the way you talk to me,' Alex said firmly. 'Once and for all, try to understand that I will not be bullied. If you thought I would just collapse, you picked the wrong person.'

'I'm only trying—'

'I know what you're "only trying" and I've heard enough. Now I'm going out. If you wish to talk to me you can make an appointment with my lawyer.'

'The hell I will!'

'The hell you won't!'

Alex snatched up her purse and made for the door. Grim-faced, he moved fast, and she thought he was going to bar her way. Instead he opened the door for her and followed her out.

In the street she walked on without looking where she was going.

'Which of them are you going to meet now?' he demanded, walking beside her.

'Well, of all the—'

'Tell me.'

'It's none of your business.'

He got in front of her, forcing her to stop. 'If you're meeting Montelli it *is* my business.'

'If and when I meet Signor Montelli it will be in my lawyer's office, which is also where I will meet you—always supposing that I *want* to meet you. Now please get out of my way. I'd like to find somewhere to eat.'

Slightly to her surprise he moved aside. 'I can recommend a good place in the next street—'

'You mean it's run by a friend of yours who'll keep an eye on me?' she said lightly.

'You're full of suspicion.'

'Shouldn't I be?'

Wryly, he nodded. 'You're also a very wise woman.'

'Wise enough to pick a restaurant for myself. Your choice might have arsenic in the wine.'

'Only if you have put me in your will.'

The last thing she'd expected from him was a joke, and a choke of laughter burst from her. She controlled it quickly, not wishing to yield a point to him.

Then she turned a corner and stopped in sudden delight at what she saw.

Before her was a huge loggia filled with stalls, selling pictures, ornaments, lace, leather goods, fancy materials. Everywhere was brightly coloured and bustling with life.

Most fascinating of all was a large bronze boar perched on a pedestal which contained a fountain, its tusks gleaming, its mouth open in a grin that mixed ferocity and welcome. Unlike the rest of the body, the nose was gleaming brightly in the late evening sun.

Even as Alex looked, two young women went up to the boar and rubbed its nose.

'That's why it shines,' Rinaldo said. 'You rub the nose and make a wish that one day you'll return to Florence.'

Smiling, Alex put out her hand, but withdrew it without touching the bronze animal.

'I'm not sure what I'll do,' she said, as though considering seriously. 'Wishing to return to Florence would mean that I was leaving, wouldn't it? And that's so much what you're trying to make me do that I think I should do the opposite.'

He eyed her with exasperation. But he did not, as she had been half hoping, show signs of real annoyance.

'Of course, if I just decide to stay here, I wouldn't need to return,' she mused.

'I suppose this entertains you,' he growled. 'To me it's a waste of time.'

'I'm sure you're right. I'll defer a decision until I've worked out what would annoy you the most.'

She began to turn away, but he grasped her upper arm with a hand that could almost encompass it. His grip was light, but she could sense the steel in his fingers, and knew that she had no chance of escape until he released her.

'And then you'll annoy me, for fun,' he said. 'But beware, *signorina*, to me this is not fun. My life's blood is in Belluna. You will remember that, and you will respect it, because if you do not—' his eyes, fixed on hers, were hard as flint '—if you do not—you will wish that you had. I have warned you.'

He removed his hand.

'Enjoy your meal,' he said curtly, and vanished into the crowd.

It was over. He was gone. All the things she ought to have said came crowding into her head now that it was too late to say them. All that was left was the imprint of his hand on the bare skin of her arm. He hadn't held her all that tightly, but she could still feel him.

She turned away from the market and walked on through the streets. She found a restaurant and entered, barely noticing her surroundings.

The food was superb, duck terrine flavoured with black truffle, chick-pea soup with giant prawn tails. She had eaten in the finest restaurants in London and New York, but this was a whole new experience. More art than food.

'Definitely, I am not going home before I have to,' she murmured. 'He can say what he likes.'

CHAPTER THREE

ALEX decided to allow herself the next day for sightseeing. It beat sitting in her room waiting to see what Rinaldo would do next.

But as she descended into the foyer the bulky form of Signor Montelli darkened the door. Alex groaned at the sight of the oily, charmless man whom she remembered from the wake. Reluctantly she sat down with him at a table in the hotel's coffee shop.

'I have come to solve your problems,' he declared loftily.

It was the wrong approach. Alex was immediately antagonised.

'I'm sure that I have no problems that you could possibly know about,' she replied coolly.

'I mean that I'm prepared to pay a high price for your mortgage on the Farnese property. I'm sure we can come to terms.'

'Perhaps we can, but not just yet. I must give the first chance to the Farnese brothers.'

He shrugged dismissively. 'They can't afford it.'

'How do you know how much it is?' she asked curiously.

'Oh—' he said airily, 'these things become known. I'm sure you want to turn your inheritance into cash as soon as possible.'

Since this was precisely why she'd come out to Italy it was unreasonable of Alex to take offence, but she found her resistance stiffening. This man was far too sure of himself.

'I'm afraid I can't discuss it with you until I've discussed it with them,' she said firmly.

He named a price.

Despite herself Alex was shaken. The money he offered was more than she was owed. The accountant in her spoke, urging her to close the deal now.

But her sense of justice intervened and made her repeat, 'I must speak to them first.'

His eyes narrowed. 'I'm not a patient man, *signorina*.'

'I'll have to take the risk of losing your offer, won't I?' she said lightly. 'Now, if you'll excuse me.'

As she rose Montelli's hand came out and grasped her wrist.

'We haven't finished talking.'

'Yes, we have,' she snapped, 'and if you don't release me right now I shall slap your face so hard that your ears will be ringing for a week.'

'Better do as she says,' Gino advised. 'Otherwise I'll get to work on you myself.'

Neither of them had seen him come into the coffee shop. Montelli scowled and withdrew his hand.

'Shall I thump him for you anyway?' Gino asked her pleasantly.

'Don't you dare!' she said firmly. 'If there's any thumping to be done I want the pleasure of doing it personally.'

Gino grinned. Then, glancing at Montelli, he said curtly, 'Take yourself off.'

The transformation in him was astonishing. Instead of the smiling boy there was a hard, steely man. Then it was over, and the pleasant young man was there again. But for a moment Alex could see that this was Rinaldo's brother.

Montelli saw it too, for he scuttled away.

'My chance to rescue a damsel in distress,' Gino said, laughing. 'And you had to spoil it. Couldn't you have pretended to be just a little bit scared for the sake of my male ego?'

'Oh, I should think your male ego is in fine healthy shape, without me buttering it up,' Alex observed, laughing with him.

'*Signorina*, you understand me perfectly,' he said.

He said 'signorina' differently to his brother, she thought, softer, almost with a caress, not grim and accusing. A natural flirt. A merry, uncomplicated lad. He would be excellent company.

'Are you going out?' he asked.

'Yes, I thought I'd do some sightseeing. I've never been to Florence before.'

'May I show you around? I'm at your service.'

'That would be nice. Let's have a coffee and discuss it.'

They found a small café near the loggia and drank coffee in sight of the bronze boar. Alex waited for him to tell her about the superstition of rubbing the beast's nose, but he did not.

But of course, she thought, *you know all about your brother's visit to me last night, how we fought, and then came here. He told you everything. This meeting was no accident.*

She smiled at Gino over the rim of her coffee cup, while her mind pursued her own thoughts.

He told you to come and find me, to see if charm worked any better than growling. Well, you are delight-

ful, my friend, and I'm happy to spend the day with you. But you don't fool me for a moment.

'Did Montelli hurt you, grabbing you like that?' Gino asked, taking her arm gently and studying it as though looking for bruises.

She barely felt his light touch. Nor could she recall the feel of Montelli's hand, unpleasant though it had been. The grasp that lingered was Rinaldo's, from the night before. Strange, she thought, how she could still feel that.

For a moment she saw his face again, intent, deadly, ready to do something desperate at any hint of a threat to what was his.

'No, Montelli didn't hurt me,' she said.

Gino held onto her just a little longer than necessary, before dropping her hand and saying, 'Let me take you to the Uffizi Gallery first. Here in Florence we have the greatest art in the world.'

Together they went around the vast gallery. Alex tried to look at all the pictures and show a proper appreciation, but it was too much for her. She felt as though great art was pursuing and attacking her.

They had lunch at a little restaurant overlooking the River Arno, with a perfect view of the Ponte Vecchio.

'I can't stop looking at the bridge,' Alex marvelled. 'All those buildings crowded onto it, making it seem so top-heavy. I keep thinking that it'll collapse into the water, but it doesn't. It's miraculous.'

'True,' Gino agreed. 'But then, all Florence is miraculous. Sixty per cent of the great art in the world is in Italy, and fifty per cent of that is in Florence. Because for the last few centuries—'

Alex hardly heard what he was saying. She was fascinated by him. Where else, she wondered, would a farmer lecture her about art?

But this was Florence, home of the Renaissance, which had produced men who were many sided, with subtle, wide-ranging minds.

'I'm sorry,' he said suddenly. 'Am I becoming a bore?'

'Not at all. You made me think of Renaissance man. I guess he's still around all these generations later.'

'Of course. That is our pride. Not that Rinaldo thinks so. He never raises his head from the land. But I think a man should have the soul of an artist even if he does get his hands dirty.'

She smiled, wondering exactly how dirty Gino's hands ever were. With Rinaldo she could believe it. He seemed to be a part of the very earth itself.

Gino regarded her sympathetically. 'I had thought to show you the Duomo after lunch, but—'

'Could we do that another time?' she begged. 'I couldn't cope with a cathedral just now.'

'Fine, let's find something less virtuous but far more fun.'

'Such as what?' she asked, eyeing him suspiciously.

'Horse riding?' he asked innocently. 'Why, what did you think I meant?'

Her lips twitched. 'Never mind. I'd love to go riding.'

Gino's glance met hers. His eyes flashed with humour, seeming to say that, yes, he'd been thinking exactly what she thought he was thinking. But that could come later.

Since she had no riding clothes a quick shopping trip was necessary. Gino had a nice eye for women's fashion, and refused to let her make a final choice until he had approved it.

At last, when she was wearing olive green trousers and a cream shirt, he nodded, saying, 'Perfect with your colouring. That's the one.'

While she paid he fetched his car to the shop. In a few

minutes they were on their way out of Florence, leading north to the hills.

At a small livery stable Gino hired a couple of horses, and they set off over the countryside. Alex was soon at home on the unfamiliar mare, who had a sweet disposition and a soft mouth.

After a good gallop they stopped in a village. The local inn had a garden, and they sat there eating fresh-baked bread and strong cheese.

'I love riding, but I haven't done any for a while,' Alex said with a sigh. 'This is wonderful.'

For the first time in days she felt totally relaxed and contented. The wildness of the scenery was alien to her, yet somehow it made her feel good.

David, she was sure, would never feel at ease here. His riding was done in the extensive grounds of his country house, on elegant animals from his own stables.

She realised suddenly that she hadn't spoken to him since she arrived. When she'd called his mobile phone had been switched off, so she had left a message.

She reached into her jacket pocket and checked her own phone, finding that it too was off. She wondered when she had done that.

She found a message from David to say that he'd called her back but been unable to get through. She dialled and found herself talking to his answering machine. After leaving a message she switched off again, returned the phone to her jacket, and looked up to find Gino watching her.

'Is he your lover?' he asked.

'*What?*'

'I'm sorry, I had no right to ask. But it's important to me to know.'

'You just want to know if I'm going to bring reinforcements out here?'

Gino shook his head. 'No, that's not what I meant. I have other reasons.'

His eyes told her what those reasons were. Alex did not speak. She wasn't sure what she would have said about David right now.

'You're like Rinaldo,' Gino said. 'He plays his cards close to his chest too.'

'Don't you dare say I'm like him!' she cried in mock indignation. 'He has no manners, and he acts like a juggernaut.'

'He really got under your skin last night, didn't he?'

'So he told you that? And how much of this meeting will you tell him about?'

She was teasing and he answered in the same vein. 'Not all of it.'

'Make sure he knows that I can be a juggernaut too.'

'I'll bet you made it plain to him yourself.'

She laughed. 'Come to think of it, yes I did.'

'You've got a lot of power, and he doesn't like other people having power, especially over him.'

'Well, it'll all be sorted out soon.'

'But how? You want your money.'

'Hey, there's no need to make me sound mercenary— even if Rinaldo thinks I am.'

'Sorry. I didn't mean it that way. But if we can't raise the money soon there'll be plenty who can, not just Montelli. Have any of the others approached you?'

Alex regarded him with her head on one side.

'Gino,' she teased, 'why don't you just tell Rinaldo not to treat me like a fool? Say you've had a wasted day.'

Gino's eyes gleamed.

'But the day isn't over yet. And, though you may not

believe it, the mortgage seems less important by the minute. There are so many other things about you that matter more.'

She gave him a smiling glance, but didn't answer in words.

They rode quietly back to the stables in the setting sun. Gino said little as he drove her back to Florence, but as he drew up outside the hotel he said, 'May I take you to dinner tonight?'

She couldn't resist saying, 'To make sure that nobody else does?'

He smiled and shook his head. 'No,' he said simply. 'Not for that reason.'

She just stopped herself from saying, 'And pigs fly!' He was a nice lad, and she was going to enjoy flirting the evening away with him. It would be different if she were fooled by his caressing ways, but she wasn't. Her heart was safe, and so, she was sure, was his.

There would be no disloyalty to David, and she might learn something useful in the coming battle.

'I'll believe you,' she teased. 'Thousands wouldn't.'

They settled that he would collect her at eight o'clock, which gave her time to find something to wear. She had thought herself well equipped with clothes, but the hotel's shopping arcade had a boutique with the latest lines from Milan.

With leisure to steep herself in Italian fashion she discovered it was unlike anything she had known before. She stepped into the shop, telling herself that she would just take a quick look. When she stepped out again she was the proud owner of a dark blue silk dress, demure in the front and low in the back, clinging on the hips.

His eyebrows went up when he saw her in the daring dress, complete with diamond earrings.

'*Signorina*,' he said softly, 'to be seen with you is an honour.'

Alex couldn't help it. She burst out laughing.

'What?' he asked in comic dismay.

'I'm sorry,' she choked. 'But I can't keep a straight face when you start that ''signorina'' stuff. I wish you'd just call me Alex, and remember that you're far more appealing when you're not trying so hard.'

'Does that mean you do find me appealing some-times?' he asked with comical pathos.

'Are you going to feed me, or are we going to stand here talking all night?' she asked severely.

'I'm going to feed you,' he said hastily. 'I've booked us a table in a place very near here. Can you walk in those shoes?'

Her long legs ended in delicate silver sandals, with high heels.

'Of course I can,' she told him. 'It's just a question of balance.' She added significantly, 'And I'm very good at doing a balancing act.'

It was a perfect evening as they strolled down to the banks of the Arno and across the Ponte Vecchio. Alex paused to look into the shops that lined the bridge. There had been goldsmiths here for centuries, and their wares were still displayed in gorgeous profusion.

As at lunchtime, they ate near the river. Now the day-light was fading, the lamps were coming on, reflected in the water, and there was a new kind of magic.

Gino was also a perfect host, surrounding her with a cocoon of comfort and consideration, entertaining her with funny stories.

She made him talk about the farm and his life there, while she ate her way through chicken liver canapés, noodles with hare sauce, and *Bistecca al la Fiorentina*, a charbroiled steak.

'It's been cooked this way since the fourteenth century,' Gino explained. 'The legend says that the town magistrates used to cook it themselves in the Palazzo Vecchio, if it was a busy day. It saved going home for lunch.'

'You made that up.'

'I swear I didn't. I don't say that it's true, but it's the legend.'

'And a good legend can be as powerful as the truth,' Alex mused.

He nodded. 'More. Because the legend tells you what people *want* to believe.'

She gave a little laugh. 'Like your brother wants to believe in me as a Wicked Witch.'

Gino regarded her wryly. 'Do you know how often you do that?' he asked.

'Do what?'

'Bring the conversation back to Rinaldo. You've convinced yourself that he's pulling my strings, and I feel as though you don't really see me at all. You're looking over my shoulder at him all the time.'

'I'm sorry,' she said quickly. 'I didn't mean to sound like that. It's just—well, perhaps you should blame him. I'm sure he likes to think of himself as pulling your strings—everyone's strings. Somehow, one takes him at his own estimation.'

'That's true,' he said with a rueful sigh. 'Let's have some champagne.'

He turned to call the waiter, leaving Alex to reflect. She was shaken by the realisation that Gino was right. While she smiled and flirted with him, Rinaldo seemed to be constantly there, an unseen but dominant presence.

When the champagne had arrived he began to reminisce once more about his childhood.

'I'll never forget the day my father brought me to Florence for the carnival in the streets. We went through it together, visiting all the stalls. He was as much a kid as I was. At least, that's what my mother always said.'

'How old were you when she died?'

'Eight.'

'How sad! And your father never remarried?'

'No, he said he never would, and he stuck to that until his own death.'

'Your father sounds like a delightful person,' she said warmly.

'He was. Of course, Rinaldo thought he was too frivolous, always joking when he should have been serious. Poppa would tease him and say, ''Lighten up, the world is a better place than you think''.'

'Now you're doing it,' she told him. 'Bringing the conversation back to Rinaldo.'

'I know. As you say, it's hard not to.'

'What did he used to say when your father teased him like that?'

'Nothing, he'd just scowl and remember something that had to be done somewhere else. I'll swear nothing matters to him but work.'

'Well, I suppose that's good in a way,' Alex said. 'The work has to be done.'

'Hey, I do my share. It's just that, like Poppa, I believe in having fun too.'

'Has Rinaldo always been gloomy?'

'He's always been serious, but it's really only since his wife died that he's actually been morose.'

'His wife?' Alex echoed, startled.

'Yes, her name was Maria. She came from Fiesole, a

tiny little town near here. They were childhood sweet-hearts. I think they got engaged when they were fifteen. They married when they were twenty.'

'What was she like?' Alex asked curiously.

She was trying to imagine the kind of woman who would attract Rinaldo, but she found it hard to picture him in love.

'She was pretty and plump and motherly. You'd prob-ably call her old-fashioned because all she wanted was to look after us. My mother was dead by then, so it was really nice having her.'

'Is that why he married her?' Alex asked, scandalised. 'To have a woman about the place?'

Gino grinned.

'Oh no! He was crazy about her. It was Poppa and me who needed motherly attention. I was ten years old. Maria was a great cook, and that's really all a ten-year-old boy cares about. She and Rinaldo seemed very happy. I used to see him come up behind her, put his arms about her and nuzzle her neck. He was a changed man. He laughed.'

'What happened?'

'They were going to have a baby, but it was born at seven months and both mother and child died.'

'Oh, heavens!' Alex whispered in horror. 'How long ago was that?'

'Fifteen years. They'd been married for less than two years.'

'How awful for him. To be so young and watch his wife die—'

'It was worse than that. He wasn't there. Nobody ex-pected the baby to come so soon, and he was away buy-ing machinery. Poppa called him as soon as things started to happen and he rushed back, but he was too late.

'I was there in the hospital when he arrived, and I'll never forget the sight of him. He'd driven all night, and he looked like a madman, with wild eyes. When the doctor told him Maria was dead he wouldn't believe it. He rushed into her room and seized her up in his arms.

'I'd never seen him cry before. I didn't think it was possible, but he was off his head.

'At that stage the baby was still alive, but not expected to live. They baptised him quickly. He wanted to hold him, but he couldn't because he had to stay in the incubator. It was no use though. He died half an hour later.

'By that time he'd calmed down but it was almost worse than when he was raving. He was in a trance, just staring and not seeing anything. He got through the funeral like that—just one funeral, with them both in the same coffin. It was almost as though he didn't know what was happening.

'Since then he never speaks of them. If I try to mention them he just blanks me out. I'm not sure what he feels now. Probably nothing. He seems to have deadened that side of him.'

'Can any man do that?' Alex mused.

'Rinaldo can. He can do whatever he sets his mind to. Why should he want to go through such pain again?'

'But surely it could never happen again? No man could be so unlucky twice.'

'I think he's decided not to take a chance on it. Since Maria died the farm has been his whole life. Poppa left the running of it to him.'

'What about you?'

Gino gave his attractive, boyish grin.

'Theoretically I have as much authority as my brother, but Rinaldo's a great one for letting you know who's the meat and who's the potatoes. His being so much older helps, of course.'

There was something slightly mechanical about Alex's smile. She no longer felt able to joke about Rinaldo. The image of the overbearing dictator that had dominated her thoughts had suddenly become blurred.

There was another image now, a young man agonising over the death of his wife and child, then growing older too fast, hardening in his despair.

'Are you all right?' Gino asked as she rubbed her hand over her eyes.

'Yes, I'm just a little tired. I'm not used to so much heat.'

'Let me take you back to the hotel.'

The night air was blessedly cool as they strolled back. To her relief he seemed in tune with her mood, and did not talk.

At the door of the hotel he took her hand and said, 'I'd ask to see you again, but you'd only think Rinaldo put me up to it. So I won't.'

She smiled. 'That's very clever.'

'But it's all right if I call you, isn't it?'

'Yes, but not tomorrow.'

He nodded. Leaning forward he kissed her cheek gently, and walked away.

Gino slipped into the house quietly, but his caution was wasted, as he had feared that it would be.

'Good evening,' Rinaldo said, without looking up from the computer screen where he was doing the accounts

'Don't you ever sleep?' Gino asked.

Rinaldo didn't answer this. Dragging his eyes away from the screen he leaned back, stretching like a man whose limbs had been cramped too long.

'You look like the cat that swallowed the cream,' he observed. 'I hope the cream was good.'

'Don't be coarse.'

'I also hope you didn't forget that you were there for a purpose. You haven't just been enjoying yourself, you were supposed to be neutralising a threat.'

'Alex is no threat. She's trying to be as helpful to us as she can.'

Rinaldo groaned.

'She really got to you, didn't she? Well, before you get too starry-eyed, remember that this is the woman who was negotiating with Montelli at our father's funeral.'

'She wasn't negotiating. He just walked up to her. In fact he did it again today and she drove him off with threats of violence. I heard her.'

'He was there again?'

'They were in the coffee shop when I arrived, and she sent him packing.'

'Of course—because she saw you.'

'You're a cynical swine, aren't you?'

'I know more about women than you do, and a damned sight more about hard cash. And one of us needs to be cynical about this lady. You're evidently a lost cause. What did she do? Flutter her eyelids and let you look deep into her blue eyes?'

'They're not exactly blue,' Gino said, considering. 'More like a kind of violet.'

'They looked ordinary blue to me.'

'Maybe you weren't looking at them in the right way.'

'I was looking at them with suspicion, and that's the right way,' Rinaldo growled.

'Well, maybe it was the dress,' Gino agreed. 'That was dark blue and very elegant, sort of clingy, especially over her waist and hips—'

Rinaldo got to his feet restively.

'I don't want to hear any more,' he growled. 'You've plainly made a fool of yourself—'

'If you mean that I'm enchanted, I plead guilty.'

'Enchanted. Listen to yourself. You were sent on a mission and you return spouting a lot of sentimental drivel. She's probably laughing at you this minute. In fact, it wouldn't surprise me if she got straight on the phone to Montelli as soon as you left.'

'You're determined to think the worst of her, aren't you?'

'With reason.'

'You know nothing about her,' Gino said with a flash of anger. 'You've been prejudiced since the first moment.'

'Do you blame me?'

'I blame you for not giving her a chance.'

Rinaldo sighed.

'But it isn't up to me. It lies in her hands now, that's what's so damned—' he checked himself.

'Don't worry,' Gino said. 'She's as crazy about me as I am about her. From now on, everything's going to be fine.'

CHAPTER FOUR

ALEX had often heard of the magic of Italy, but, being a practical person, she had dismissed it as romanticising. Now she found that it was real.

Perhaps it was in the light that intensified every colour. Or perhaps it was Florence, packed with medieval buildings, where there were as many cobblestones as modern roads.

She tried not to be seduced by the beauty. She was only here to raise money, then return to London, marriage to David, the partnership: in other words, her 'real' life.

It was just that it seemed less real suddenly, and she could feel no hurry to push things along. David had told her to take as much time as she needed, and it might be better to stay here for a while, and broaden her mind.

So the day after her meeting with Gino, she did something she hadn't done for years. She played hookey.

Firmly turning off her mobile phone she hired a car and left Florence, heading south. After a few miles she began to climb until she reached the tiny, ancient town of Fiesole.

After wandering its cobbled streets for an hour, she found a restaurant with tables on a balcony looking far down, and sat there, sipping coffee and gazing at the rows of cypresses, and the elegant villas that were laid out before her.

'You're in good company,' said a quiet voice.

Rinaldo had appeared, seemingly from nowhere. She

wondered how long he had been standing there, watching her.

But today, although his face was grave, there was no antagonism in it as he came to sit at her table.

'Good company?' she asked.

'Your English writers, Shelley and Dickens, once admired this valley. Down there is the villa where Lorenzo de Medici entertained his literary friends. This little town is known as the mother of Florence. Look around and you'll see why.'

Alex saw it at once. The whole panorama of Florence, barely five miles away, was spread out before them, glowing in the noon haze, the great Duomo rising out of a sea of roofs, dwarfing everything else.

'What are you doing up here?' he asked lightly.

'Do I need your permission?'

'Not at all, but wouldn't you be better occupied negotiating? You're a woman of business. There's work to be done, and here you are, wasting time, staring into the distance.'

Alex didn't normally quote poetry, but this time she couldn't resist it.

'What is this life if, full of care,

We have no time to stand and stare?'

Rinaldo frowned. 'Who said that?'

'An English poet.'

'An *Englishman?*' he demanded on an unflattering emphasis.

'Yes,' she said, nettled. 'Strange as it may seem, an Englishman wrote it. Shock! Horror! Now you might have to adjust your ideas about the English.

'You think of me holding court, receiving my financial suitors one by one, selling you out to the highest bidder. And let's face it, that's how you prefer to see me.'

Rinaldo hailed a passing waiter and ordered two coffees. Alex had an amused feeling that he was giving himself a breathing space to come to terms with her attack.

'You were probably following me up here,' she added, 'to see if I met up with a prospective buyer behind your back.'

'No, I've been visiting friends in Fiesole. This is pure chance.'

Suddenly she remembered that Gino had said his wife came from this town, and wondered if he had been to see Maria's family.

'Anyway, you're wrong,' she said in a gentler tone. 'I have nothing to negotiate, not with Montelli or anyone else of his kind, until I've first talked seriously with you. Anyway, I dislike him.'

Rinaldo gave her a grin that was as harsh as it was humorous. 'The question is, do you dislike him as much as you dislike me?'

'I haven't quite decided, but it makes no difference. I never allow personalities to interfere with business.'

'Like a good accountant?' he mocked.

'No, like a civilised human being actually,' she said crisply.

He gave a half nod, acknowledging a hit to her.

The coffees were served, giving them both a brief time out.

'I wonder what your notion of "civilised" includes,' he mused when they were alone again. 'My brother?'

'Your brother is a nice lad, but I told him, and I'm telling you, don't treat me like a fool.'

'Meaning?'

'Meaning that you should have been ashamed to be so obvious. You sent him out to say pretty nothings to me because you thought I was a ninny who'd faint the moment an Italian gave her the eye. Well, he's delightful and he made my head spin—not perhaps as much as you planned, but enough for a very nice day.

'But let me make one thing plain to you, Signor Farnese. I do not make serious decisions while my head is spinning. I hope that's clear.'

He began to laugh, a robust, virile sound that was free from strain. He could be really attractive, she realised; a man, in contrast to his brother's boyishness.

'I see that Gino has been fooling himself,' he said. 'This isn't the impression I got from him.'

There was a silence, during which they eyed each other. Alex smiled.

'Signor Farnese, if you're waiting for me to ask what he said about me, you'll wait for ever.'

He raised his eyebrows. 'You're not interested in knowing?'

'Let's just say that I have exceptional self-control.'

He inclined his head in salute.

'My compliments, *signorina*. You fight with courage and skill. Poor Gino. I'm afraid you'll break his heart.'

'I don't think there's any fear of that! He knew the nature of the duel. His heart isn't involved any more than mine.'

'Don't be too sure of that. Gino is a man who gives his affections easily. In that, he is not like me, or you.'

'You know nothing about me.'

'Only what you've just told me, which is that you're a woman who likes to be in control—'

'Just like you.'

'Just like me. Also like me, your head rules your heart. I respect that, but it makes me wary of you.'

'You mean I'm not going to be the simple-minded walkover that you were expecting.'

'I don't think I would ever call you simple-minded,' he said gravely. 'May I buy you lunch?'

'No, thank you. I've had a snack and it's time for me to be going.'

'Let me walk with you to your car.'

She led the short distance to where she had parked, and as soon as he saw her car he grimaced.

'What's wrong?' she demanded.

'I know this car. I know the firm you hired it from. Neither are reliable.'

As if to prove it, the car made forlorn choking noises and refused to budge.

'Oh, great!' she said, exasperated. 'How do I start this?'

'You don't. You'll have to abandon it and tell the firm to come for it later.'

Muttering, she got out and called the hire firm on her mobile phone. The ensuing conversation was terse on both sides. The firm was reluctant to accept responsibility, insisting that the car had been perfect when consigned to her, and that it was her job to get it back.

As the argument grew heated she saw, to her annoyance, that Rinaldo was observing and taking in everything. At last, with the air of a man who could endure no more, he reached over, took the phone from her and spoke into it sharply and in Tuscan.

The effect was instantaneous. As she recovered the phone and put it to her ear the man on the other end was burbling with eagerness to please. Alex couldn't decide whether she was more relieved to have the business sorted, or exasperated at being beholden to Rinaldo. His grin told her that he understood her dilemma perfectly.

'Thank you,' she said crisply. 'I'm grateful to you.'

'No you're not,' he said cheerfully. 'You'd like to murder me.'

'I'm far too much of a lady to say so.'

The phone rang before she could switch it off. She answered, turning away slightly.

'Alex?' It was David's voice.

'Hello, darling.'

'I got your message. Sorry I couldn't call back before. How are you doing out there?'

'It has its ups and downs.'

'I take it the arrangements are problematic?'

'Very,' she said. 'But I'll get there.'

'Are the Farnese brothers being difficult?'

'Nothing I can't cope with,' she said, loud enough for Rinaldo to hear.

'Don't stand for it,' David told her. 'You hold all the cards.'

'Well, I know that. But everything isn't as simple as it seemed when we were talking in England.'

'If they start making themselves unpleasant, just set the lawyers onto them.'

'It's sweet of you to worry about me,' she said tenderly, 'but honestly darling, I'm coping really well.'

'Hm! Well, I suppose that's true. I know how efficient you always are.'

Alex made a wry face. As a tribute 'efficient' lacked something. But David had never been a man for emotional pronouncements. Once she had liked that about him. Now it struck a jarring note.

'Just leave everything to me,' she said.

He laughed suddenly. 'I begin to feel sorry for them. They don't know what they've taken on.'

She joined in his laughter, but she would have preferred to hear it put some other way.

'Take as long as you need,' David said. 'I've got your work here covered so you don't need to give it another thought.'

'Thank you, but of course I think about it all the time. And you. It'll be lovely getting back to you.'

'We're going to have a lot to talk about,' he assured her.

Rinaldo heard her laughter and it chilled him. Without consciously eavesdropping—so he told himself—he had contrived to hear enough to alarm him.

This man was a lover, in her thoughts all the time. She called him 'darling' and longed to return to him.

He began to appreciate the true dimensions of the threat to everything he held dear, and he called himself a fool for underestimating the danger.

His eyes narrowed as he came to a swift resolution. Alex was hanging up, turning back to him, and he swung away from her so that she shouldn't see his thoughts reflected in his face.

When he was ready to face her again he was smiling.

'Come,' he said, taking her hand. 'This way to my car.'

'I can't go with you. I have to stay here for the breakdown truck.'

'Nonsense. Just leave the keys in the ignition. Nobody can steal it, since the car can't move. Now come on.'

He was making his way to a car on the far side of the parking lot.

'Come where?' she asked.

She tried to pull away but his grip, although light, was unbreakable.

'There are things you need to see.'

'Will you let me go?'

'No, I won't. So don't waste time asking me.'

'This is kidnap,' she seethed.

'You can call it what you like.'

It would have been easy to scream for help, and rouse some passer-by to assist her. Alex could never quite understand why she didn't do this.

She was still considering the matter as he opened the door of his vehicle for her to get in.

The car was a heavy four-wheel drive, long past its best, but suitable for rough terrain. Swinging out of Fiesole they were soon at the bottom of the slope and heading for the great hills she could see looming ahead, waiting for them.

'Are you going to show me Belluna?' she asked.

'Some of it. There's too much to see in one go. But it's time you saw what you're negotiating about.'

Soon they began to climb again. Florence vanished. The land grew wild, fierce, somehow darker, yet filled with violent colour. Had there ever been such colours, she wondered?

'Stop a moment,' she said.

Rinaldo halted the car, and she immediately opened the door and jumped out.

'Careful!' he cried. 'It's steep here. But you picked a good place.'

They were up high, looking far out over the valley and the far hills. The sun streamed down over the scene, touching fields, full of flourishing crops. Far off there was a village, its red roofs and glinting windows also bathed in warmth and light.

Alex took a deep breath, filling her lungs with the pure fresh air, without a trace of city fumes.

She was city born and bred, and had always regarded London as her natural home. But in these wide spaces she suddenly felt free to breathe, as if for the first time.

'Over there are the vineyards,' Rinaldo said, coming

beside her. 'See, on that steep slope, with the vines arranged in tiers so that they all catch as much of the sun as possible.

'We also grow wheat and olives, but I dare say the lawyers have told you all that.'

'I've seen it all written down in columns,' she agreed. 'But this—is so different.'

'This is just cash to you, but to us the land is a living, breathing creature that works with us to create new life. Then again, sometimes it works against us, even tries to kill us. But it belongs to us, as we belong to it.'

She mopped her brow. It was the hottest part of the day.

'Come over here,' he said, taking her arm and leading her to where a stream plunged downhill. There were a few trees in this spot, giving a blessed shade.

'Maybe I shouldn't have brought you here just now,' he said. 'You're not used to this kind of heat.'

'I'm very tough,' she assured him.

'You don't look it. You look as if a breeze would blow you away.'

She laughed and made a gesture to indicate the still air. 'What breeze?'

'Sit down,' he said, urging her to the water's edge.

His own face and neck were damp with perspiration. He pulled out a clean handkerchief and dropped it into the stream, then squeezing the water over himself. Alex tried to do the same, but her handkerchief was too small to be effective.

'Here,' he said, soaking his again and passing it to her.

She buried her face in it, grateful for the relief, then drenched it again. When she had finished she found him looking at her.

She guessed he was watching for some sign of weakness. If so, he would be disappointed. She had her second wind now and knew that this was something she could deal with, even relish. The sheer ferocity of the elements in this country had lit a small flame of excitement in her. Go now, warned a voice in her head. Before it grows and takes you over.

She laid her hand against the earth, moving her fingers to feel it against her.

'Not like that,' he said quietly. 'Dig in deep, and really feel it. Let it speak to you.'

She tried it, and knew at once what he meant. Here by the stream the earth was springy, damp and crumbling. From it came a lush, powerful odour that was not unpleasant.

Speaking almost in a daze she said, 'You could grow anything in this.'

His answer came without words. Plunging his own hand into the ground he raised it to show her. She touched it, and at once he gripped her hand, pressing it into the rich earth that he was holding.

It felt good, and the sense of power in his hands beneath the living soil made her strangely giddy.

'You see?' he said intently. *'You see?'*

'Yes,' she whispered. 'I see.'

Something seemed to have taken possession of her. She didn't want to open her fingers. She had the impression that the sun had darkened, but instead of blotting out her surroundings it made them more vivid.

There was a big scar on the back of his hand. She couldn't take her eyes away from it.

Then he moved, prising her fingers open and drawing her hand gently down into the cleansing water.

'It's time we were going,' he said quietly.

She nodded, rubbing the earth away, past speech.

When she was sitting beside him in the car he turned it and began the journey back down the track to where the road forked. There was a signpost, showing the way to Florence, but he swung away.

'Where are we going?' she asked.

'I'm taking you home.'

'Home?'

'My home.'

She didn't let him see how much this pleased her. She was more curious to see Rinaldo's home than she would admit.

She had pictured a shabby, weather-beaten farmhouse, but the building that finally came into view had a touch of grandeur. It was three stories high, with a double staircase that formed two curves up the front.

But what really amazed her was that it was made of a stone that appeared pink in the red-gold of the setting sun. At that moment the sun shone directly into her eyes, making her blink, and giving the building the appearance of a frosted cake.

She blinked again and the world righted itself. It was just a house, although still more ornate than any farmhouse she had ever seen.

'It's beautiful,' she breathed.

'Yes,' he agreed. 'At one time it was what I supposed you'd call a great house, but the man who owned it two hundred years ago fell on hard times. He had to sell off some of his land, and start farming the rest.

'The place has changed hands several times. My grandfather bought it and worked himself into the grave to make it prosper. My father gave his whole life to it as well.'

'And you live in that beautiful house?'

'Part of it. The rest is shut up. Teresa, who looks after

us, complains about how hard it is to keep even a small part clean.'

A door at ground level was pulled open from the inside, but, instead of Teresa, Alex saw a vast dog, of miscellaneous parentage, come lumbering out.

He might have been part Great Dane, part Alsatian. He might have been a St Bernard crossed with a lurcher. He might have been anything.

He ambled towards them obviously so excited to see them that he was getting dangerously near the vehicle. Rinaldo was forced to brake sharply.

A stream of fierce words came from him. The dog either didn't understand or didn't care because he reared up to put his head through Rinaldo's window and cover him with eager licks.

'That's enough,' Rinaldo growled, but he didn't push the animal away. 'This ridiculous object is Brutus,' he informed Alex. 'He thinks he's mine. Or I'm his. One of the two.'

He tweaked the animal's ears and said, *'Vai via!'* pointing into the distance.

Reluctantly Brutus moved back. But as soon as they were out of the car he surged forward again, this time at Alex.

She gave a yell of alarm. The next moment she was looking down at her elegant pants, now displaying a large, dirty paw print.

She opened her mouth, but her exclamation was checked by the sight of the dog, beaming at her, clearly convinced that he had done something brilliant.

'It would be a waste of time saying anything to you, wouldn't it?' she demanded, pointing to the smudge.

He woofed agreement.

'Then I won't bother,' she said, smiling despite herself. 'But if you do it again—'

He waited, grinning foolishly.

'If you do it again—' she sighed, recognising defeat '—then I guess I'll just have to forgive you again.'

Ecstatic at this appreciation, Brutus reared up and placed another mark next to the first.

'My apologies,' Rinaldo said, sounding strained. *'Brutus!'*

'Oh, don't be mad at him,' Alex said. 'He was only being friendly. I suppose he's made that way.'

'No, he doesn't usually take to strangers. He's never done that before. Naturally I'll pay the cost of cleaning.'

Alex shook her head. The sight of Rinaldo at a disadvantage was improving her mood.

'I shouldn't bother,' she said. 'It won't clean.'

'Then I will pay for a replacement,' he said stiffly.

Alex began to laugh. 'Don't force me to tell you how much it cost,' she said. 'I don't want to spoil your supper.'

He regarded her oddly. 'You're being very nice about it.'

'And that's really got you puzzled, hasn't it? If I'm being nice, it must be for an evil purpose. Forget it for heaven's sake! A dog is a dog is a dog. Making a mess is what dogs do.'

Now she had really wrong-footed him, she saw with pleasure. He was no longer quite so certain what to think of her, and that confused him.

Good! The longer she could keep him confused the better.

Teresa appeared. She was elderly, with white hair and sharp blue eyes that flickered quickly over Alex.

'Teresa, this is Signorina Dacre, from England. Enrico Mori was her great-uncle.'

'*Buon giorno, signorina.*'

'*Buon giorno, Teresa,*' Alex responded.

He introduced Alex, who saw the briefest reaction flicker across the housekeeper's face. She wondered how freely the brothers had discussed her, and what Teresa had overheard.

'Let's go inside,' Rinaldo said. 'The *signorina* has been out in the heat for too long. Show her to the guest room, please, Teresa.'

The walls of the house were thick enough to keep out the heat. The old-fashioned room was blessedly cool, and half an hour was enough to restore Alex to herself. She was feeling cheerful as she went downstairs to be shown into a room at the back of the house.

At the far end were tall windows that opened onto a veranda. A table stood just outside the room, laden with small snacks. Rinaldo was there. He looked up as she entered.

'Are you feeling better?' he asked pleasantly.

'Yes thank you. Mind you, I never did feel actually bad, just—a little overwhelmed. It was suddenly so—'

She found that she couldn't finish. No words were adequate.

Rinaldo nodded without speaking, and she knew that he understood everything she was trying to say.

He poured her a glass of light *prosecco* wine, and she sipped, glad to find it ice-cold.

Now the weather was cooling and they could sit on the veranda, while Teresa served them a sweet, crusted pie with macaroni and meat sauce, which he told her was called *Pasticcio alla Fiorentina*.

'Are you wise to treat me like this?' she teased. 'You might make me want to stay.'

'What about the man who called you? Isn't he yearning for you to return?'

She gave a choke of laughter. There was something about the idea of David yearning that was irresistibly comic.

'What is it?' he asked, watching her.

'David isn't like that. Yearning isn't his way.'

'What is his way?'

'Well—I don't know—'

'But you're in love with him?'

'Yes—no—it's none of your business.'

'As long as I'm in your power, everything about you is my business.'

'I see no need to discuss David.'

'Is he a painful subject?'

'No, he isn't. It's just that our relationship is—difficult to describe—'

'You mean it isn't passionate,' he said calmly.

'I mean nothing of the kind.'

'Then it is passionate? His kisses inflame you, your body aches for him when you are apart?'

Alex's lips twitched. Her sense of humour was coming to her rescue.

'You forget,' she said, 'that I'm a cold-blooded northerner. We don't ''do'' passion. It gets in the way of business.'

His eyes gleamed. 'A remark like that is pure provocation.'

'You can take it any way you like. David is the man I'm going to marry, and I refuse to discuss our relationship any further.'

He was silent for a long moment after that. Alex knew

that the announcement of her impending marriage was like a glove thrown down in defiance, warning him that she had her own agenda. But his face was slightly averted, and she couldn't discern what effect it had had on him.

At last he raised his head and spoke.

'Teresa is ready to serve the next course. I hope you're hungry.'

CHAPTER FIVE

TERESA served game bird cooked with Marsala wine and juniper berries. It was delicious and Alex soon persuaded herself that arguments could wait.

Sitting on the veranda they could see the light fade from the land and the sun turn deep red before sliding down the sky. Here and there a cloud seemed lit by crimson from behind.

Brutus moved between them, begging. To Alex's surprise Rinaldo showed no impatience, but fed the old dog patiently, although he advised her, 'Don't let him pester you.'

'I don't mind being pestered,' Alex said with perfect truth. 'He's beautiful.'

'He's a dog,' Rinaldo said with a touch of curtness. 'Come on, boy.'

He pushed his chair back abruptly and went into the house, calling Brutus, who followed docilely. Alex wondered about his sudden change of mood, as though she had offended him by petting his dog.

But when he returned a few moments later he seemed to have forgotten the matter.

'It's good that we have a chance to talk,' he said. 'I understand your situation better now. So, you plan to marry this David, and that's why you need money.'

'No, I need it to buy my partnership in the firm,' she said. 'David's an accountant too. It's one of the top firms in London, so a partnership comes expensive.'

She waited for him to make some sharp remark, but he only nodded, as if considering.

'How well did you know Enrico?' he asked.

'Not well at all, although he was very fond of my mother, and she talked about him a lot. In fact she talked about Italy a lot. She told me so much about Tuscany that when I got here it was like coming to a place I'd always known. She even raised me to speak Italian as well as English.'

Rinaldo frowned as though trying to remember something.

'What was your mother's name?'

'Berta.'

'Was she short and dainty with reddish hair?'

'That's right. You knew her?'

'I met her once, years ago. Enrico brought her to a party here. I was about seven and she was grown up, but she was great fun. I had this dice game that I insisted on playing with everyone until they were ready to scream.

'She sat down with me and we played and played and played. She was a mean dice player, and she had a wonderful giggle. She beat me hollow. She went to England a couple of months later and I never saw her again. So you're Berta's daughter.'

'But you must always have known this?' Alex pointed it out.

'I suppose I did know it at the back of my mind, but it's only just come to the forefront. I must have been too angry to think straight.'

'Does that make me less of an enemy?'

He considered.

'Can you play dice?'

They both laughed.

'Tell me some more about her,' he said.

'Mamma was very hot-tempered and dramatic. We didn't understand each other but we loved each other. I think I'm beginning to understand her better now.'

'Already? You've only been here a few days.'

'I know. But it's not a matter of working it out in my head. It's something I'm breathing in with the air. How could anyone be cool, calm and collected in this place?'

Rinaldo nodded. 'You can't. And we're not.'

'Surely there must be some Italians who are moderate and reasonable?' Alex said in a teasing voice.

He smiled. 'There may be one or two, hiding in corners.'

'Probably ashamed to show their faces.'

'Undoubtedly. Italy was built on passion, not reason. Moderation didn't create those great buildings and great paintings that you've seen in Florence. Passion created them, and everything else worth having, food, wine, beauty—you will find none of these sitting behind a desk.'

'Meaning me. But isn't there also a kind of beauty in good order?'

She had expected him to brush this aside, but to her surprise he nodded.

'Yes,' he said. 'But not if it's the only thing in your life.'

She would have defended herself against this slur, but somehow the words wouldn't come. What came into her mind instead was the picture of herself at her desk, at her computer, hurrying from one meeting to another in a grey, air-conditioned building from which fresh air, and anything else that was natural, had been shut out.

And the carefully scheduled time with David. All part of her life's plan. Good order. But beauty?

The sun was throwing out its last fires of gold and

crimson, drifting slowly down the sky. Its glow fell on her, and on Rinaldo. She felt not only its warmth but a feeling of contentment.

It might be wiser to resist that feeling, she thought drowsily. But for the moment she had no will to resist.

Far off in the distance she could see something moving. After a moment she made out Gino's car, heading towards them, growing larger every moment.

When he was close to the house he waved before sweeping around to the side and vanishing.

She liked Gino, but at this moment she found herself wishing he had stayed away a little longer. He could only be an intrusion in the magical atmosphere that was pervading her.

How strange, she thought, that it should be Rinaldo who was here with her, part of the magic. The man who had shown her only his harsh, formidable side was now relaxed and pleasant.

To her relief, Gino didn't join them at once. Teresa served fruits in syrup followed by black, sweet coffee.

'Now here is beauty,' Alex agreed.

'I'll tell Teresa you said so. She will appreciate it.'

'I'll tell her myself, just before I leave.'

'Yes,' he said after a moment.

'I must be going soon, I suppose. I want an early night, to be ready for Enrico's funeral tomorrow. His family are making a big "do" of it.'

'Aren't you part of his family?'

'Well yes, but you know what I mean. The people who live out here and knew him. And let me tell you, *they* don't consider me as part of the family. They're as angry with me as you are.'

'I'm not angry with you, as I hope I've made clear today. Belluna has gained much prosperity from the money my father borrowed, and it's your right to be repaid.'

Alex wrinkled her nose.

'I don't like talk of "rights",' she said, wondering at herself even as she said it.

In the world she had left behind, the world of desks and good order, rights were the markers by which everything was organised. You were entitled to this, you weren't entitled to that. And so you always knew where you stood in the universe.

But here the universe was a flood of gold spread over the land. And rights seemed unimportant.

'I suppose Enrico's funeral will turn out the same way your father's did,' she said. 'The vultures will converge on me.'

'I think I have a way to prevent that happening,' Rinaldo mused.

Before she could ask what he meant Gino appeared, greeting her eagerly, kissing her cheek.

'I'm so glad,' he said. 'When Rinaldo told me, I couldn't believe it.'

'Told you what?'

'Why, that you'd come to stay, of course.'

'But I haven't come to stay. I'm about to return to Florence, if someone will give me a lift.'

In the silence Gino looked at Rinaldo, who shrugged with an air that was almost sheepish. At any other time this would have amused her, but now a rising tide of suspicion was overtaking her, making her get to her feet to confront him.

'But I just finished bringing your bags,' Gino protested.

She whirled on him.

'And why would you do that?'

'Because Rinaldo said—hey, brother, you wouldn't! Would you?'

'Would you like to bet money on that?' Alex seethed.

'Look,' Rinaldo said, 'it's right for you to stay here awhile, and learn to understand this place.'

'OK. That makes sense. But why couldn't you have simply asked me?'

'You might have said no,' he declared flatly, as if the question were too obvious to need an answer.

'I *am* saying no. I absolutely refuse to stay here now.'

'But Teresa is in your room right now, unpacking your bags,' Gino said in dismay.

'And that's another thing,' Alex told him furiously. 'How did you come to have my luggage? I never packed it.'

'The hotel did that,' Gino said. 'They had everything ready for me.'

'And who told them to?'

Gino held up his hands, backing away as if to say that this wasn't his fault.

'I did,' Rinaldo said. 'I called them and said you weren't returning, and would they please have your things ready.'

'And did you pay my bill as well, or weren't they worried about that little matter?'

'You may recall that you signed a credit card docket when you arrived. It was simply a matter of putting it through. But I doubt if they would have worried anyway. The manager is an old friend of mine.'

'And would have jumped to obey your orders?' Alex said angrily.

Rinaldo shrugged. 'There was no need to give him orders. He knows I can be trusted. And, as I said, he already had your signature.'

'Suppose I want to dispute something on the bill?'

'You can do that tomorrow.'

'I'll do it now. I refuse to stay here. You must be quite mad.' She faced Gino, eyes glinting. 'I thought better of you.'

'But I didn't know, truly,' he pleaded. 'I thought you'd agreed.'

'Will you take me back to Florence? Or must I call for a taxi?'

'Of course I'll take you back,' he said at once.

'Forget that idea,' Rinaldo growled.

'I won't forget it,' Gino said firmly. 'Rinaldo, what are you thinking about?'

'I'm thinking about how all this is going to end,' he shouted.

'And making everyone dance around like puppets on the end of your strings,' Alex snapped. 'What did you think I'd do when I found out? Tamely submit to your decree and let you take me prisoner? If you did, you were wrong.'

'Take you prisoner? Don't be melodramatic.'

'What else would you call it?'

'*I'd* call it taking a lady prisoner,' Gino observed. 'Alex, I'll drive you back to Florence.'

At that defiance Rinaldo flung him a look that Alex never forgot. It contained rage, betrayal, disbelief, and a curious sense of hurt that she couldn't help seeing, even then.

'Gino,' Rinaldo warned, 'don't take anyone's side against me.'

'Then don't force a battle about this,' Gino said in a harsher voice than Alex had heard from him before. 'It's gone too far. You're always the same. You lose your temper and you forget everything else. Too many people jump to do as you say, but Alex doesn't. That's what's got you mad.'

Rinaldo didn't reply in words, but his look was terrible.

'Do as you like,' he said curtly.

Gino swung around to face Alex.

'I don't want you to leave,' he said quietly, 'but if that's your wish, I'm ready to take you back now.'

Alex put her hand in his.

'Do you really want me to stay?'

'More than anything, but not against your will.'

'Gino, I'm happy to remain here if I'm asked nicely and not steamrollered.'

He grinned and dropped to his knee, holding her hand between his.

'Alex, will you honour us by being our guest for as long as you wish?'

'I accept,' she said hastily, fearing that Rinaldo would explode if this went on. He was regarding them both with an air of grim exasperation.

'For pity's sake,' he snapped. 'If you mean to stay, what's the fuss about?'

'You really don't know, do you?' Alex demanded.

'No, he doesn't,' Gino confirmed.

Rinaldo scowled at him.

'If you gentlemen have finished,' Alex said, thoroughly fed up with both of them, 'I'll go upstairs to my room.'

She stormed out.

Teresa had just finished hanging her clothes up, and was preparing to take some away, to iron out the creases.

'I'll do that,' Alex said, speaking Italian.

'Oh, no!' Teresa was shocked. 'You are the mistress.'

'Don't let Rinaldo hear you say that,' Alex muttered. 'Otherwise he may murder me before I murder him.'

She couldn't have explained the annoyance that possessed her. Rinaldo had behaved badly but, with Gino's help, she'd gained the upper hand. The matter should be over.

But it wasn't over while she remembered how he'd set out to take her off guard, and how thoroughly he'd succeeded.

He'd smiled and she'd responded, and in no time at all she'd succumbed to the spell he was weaving. She hadn't even put up a good fight. The moment by the stream, the memories of her mother, even the sunset. He'd known just the right buttons to push, and she'd fallen for it hook, line and sinker.

That must have given him a laugh.

Pushing him firmly out of her head, she took a good look around the room and liked what she saw. It was out of another age, with dark oak furniture and a polished wooden floor. It had none of the modern conveniences of her bedroom at home, expensively designed and tailored to her exact specifications. But she loved it.

There was still some light outside, although it was fading fast. Driven by a sudden impulse, she slipped out of the door, down the stairs and outside.

After the heat of the day the air was blessedly cool and she stood drinking it in.

'Are you still talking to me?'

She turned, laughing, at the sound of Gino's voice.

'You're not the one I'm mad at,' she told him. 'Quite the reverse.'

'That sounds hopeful.'

'I mean that you helped me out. I really like the idea of staying here, but after the way your brother behaved, well—if you hadn't done your going-down-on-one-knee act, I'd have had to leave, simply to make my point.'

'It wasn't an act,' he said at once. 'In my heart I'm always down on one knee to you.'

'Stop your nonsense,' she told him amiably, 'or I'll take you seriously, and then where would you be?'

'In heaven! All right, I take it back if you don't like it. Let me show you the stables. There's a horse there that would just suit you.'

As they started to walk there was the sound of pattering from behind them, and the next moment Brutus wandered out, making for Alex.

'Hey,' she said, fondling his ears and trying to dodge his madly licking tongue. 'All right, don't eat me. All right, all right!'

She nuzzled him, burying her face pleasurably against his soft fur.

'He was Maria's,' Gino said. 'She brought him with her to the wedding, as a puppy. He's very old now, but Rinaldo spends a fortune on keeping him alive and fit. He's got arthritis, but as long as he has expensive injections every month, it's kept at bay. I'll swear he spends more on Brutus than he does on himself.'

Alex remembered how Rinaldo had driven the dog inside when she'd tried to make a fuss of him. She'd put it down to irritation, but now she saw the action in a new light; possessiveness about the only living creature that still reminded him of his wife.

But it had been years. How long could a man mourn?

Gino led her through the trees to where there was a long, low building, with cars parked in one section and horses housed in another.

Switching on the light, he led her into the stables where three animals looked at them curiously.

'That big brute at the end is Rinaldo's,' Gino said, pointing to a fierce-looking horse. 'This one is mine, and this third one is a kind of spare. I think you'd like him.'

He was a chestnut with mild eyes, and Alex did like him.

'We'll go out tomorrow,' Gino said, 'in the late afternoon, when we're back from the funeral, and it's cooler.'

As they left the stable he slipped an arm around her waist and drew her close, managing to drop a light kiss on her mouth.

'Behave yourself,' she said, escaping and running back to the house.

Laughing, he followed her, managing to catch up just by the porch lamp.

'You're a hard-hearted woman,' he complained. 'Or shall I go down on one knee again?'

'Don't be a fool,' she said tenderly. 'And let me go. It's time I was in bed.'

His answer was too tighten his arms and steal another kiss, but he did it with such delicacy that she couldn't be annoyed. He was like a playful puppy who only needed some affection to make him quiet again.

'Alex,' he murmured after a while, 'Couldn't we—?'

'No, we couldn't,' she said firmly. 'Now, that's enough. I'm an engaged woman.'

'But if you weren't, you and I—'

'I said that's enough,' she said, trying not to laugh.

'Just one more kiss.'

He managed to sneak one before she got away and ran indoors. Gino took a deep breath of joy, throwing back his head so that when he opened his eyes he was looking directly at the moon.

'Hm!'

The wry grunt from overhead made him turn and see his brother standing at an open window.

'I suppose you saw everything?' he asked.

'Enough!' Rinaldo growled.

'She loves me. She loves me.'

'Go to bed,' Rinaldo said, shutting his window firmly.

Enrico's funeral was scheduled for the next day at two o'clock in the great Duomo. His Florence relatives had insisted on that location as the only one suitable for a man of his prominence.

During the morning Rinaldo said to Alex, 'I imagine you'll wish to bring your luggage into town so that you can check back into the hotel.'

'Now, why would I want to do that?'

'I gathered you were only too anxious to depart.'

'That was before Gino asked me so nicely to stay. I found his invitation irresistible.'

Her ironic tone left no doubt that this was a challenge. It provoked Rinaldo to say softly, 'Do not play games with me.'

'I'm not playing games. I'm accepting an invitation that you yourself were the first to issue. You do remember that, don't you?'

He glowered without replying, and she sensed that this kind of duelling talk set him at a disadvantage. If he could have simply thrown her into the car he would have done so. As it was, they were now fighting on her terms.

'You know, you might actually regret bringing me here,' she mused, giving him a teasing smile.

'I regret it already,' he growled.

'Is everything all right?' Gino asked, appearing suddenly.

'Everything's fine,' Alex assured him. 'Rinaldo was

just hoping that I'd had a good night, and would want to make a really long stay.'

'And you know that's what I want, too,' Gino said, slipping an arm about her waist. 'Promise that you're going to stay.'

'For as long as you want me,' she assured him.

Rinaldo walked away without another word.

The three of them travelled to Florence. As they entered the Duomo heads turned towards them. She saw Montelli and the chagrined look that crossed his face at the sight of them together.

This was what Rinaldo had meant about keeping the others away. Alex smiled. Now she'd recovered from her annoyance she was almost grateful to him—almost, but not quite—for doing her a service.

At the reception afterwards her lawyer, Isidoro, approached her.

'I've promised a dozen people that you'll talk to them,' he said.

'Of course—later. Much later.'

'But look—'

'I told you, and you can tell them, the Farnese brothers have to have their chance first.'

He dropped his voice.

'I saw them arrive with you, one each side like warders. Are they keeping you prisoner?'

Alex shook her head, her eyes gleaming with mischief.

'Actually,' she said, 'it's the other way around. I've got my own agenda.'

'Do the Farneses know what it is?'

'They think they do. Get rid of the vultures for me Isidoro. Tell them I'll get round to them if and when it suits me.'

She would have escaped right then, but her cousins

descended on her with eager protestations of affection. When Alex rejoined the brothers a few minutes later she was smiling.

'What's so funny?' Rinaldo wanted to know.

'They all invited me to dinner. I said yes, as long as I could bring the two of you.' She chuckled. 'That put them right off.'

A shout of laughter was surprised from Rinaldo.

'We'll go one better and invite them all ourselves,' he suggested.

'I couldn't advise them to accept,' Alex said. 'I don't know what you might put in the soup. Or then again—maybe I do.'

Rinaldo grinned at her. It had a touch of the conspirator.

CHAPTER SIX

GOING down to an early breakfast next morning Rinaldo found his brother standing at the landing window gazing out at something that was enjoying his full attention.

'Any excuse not to start work,' he said.

'Well that is quite some excuse,' Gino said, not taking his eyes from the figure running through the trees.

At first Rinaldo saw only a flash of scarlet. Then it resolved itself into a slim, perfectly honed female body, clad in tight-fitting scarlet shorts that smoothed their way over her hips almost down to her knees, gleaming with every movement she made.

Above a bare midriff she wore a matching scarlet sports brà that left no doubts as to the beauty of her figure.

This was Alex's daily workout, and she was running with great intensity, her eyes fixed just ahead, breathing steadily and powerfully.

The brothers watched as she headed for the barn and went inside. After exchanging puzzled frowns they went downstairs and out in the direction of the barn.

They soon saw what had made her choose this place. Part of the barn was only one storey high, and the ceiling was crossed from side to side with wooden beams. To one of these Alex had attached hanging rings and was swinging along from one to the other hand over hand. A bale of hay just below showed how she had managed to launch herself up there.

Inch by inch she swung along the rings. At the end

78

she turned and started the journey back, heading for the bale where she could land easily.

But then Gino was there, kicking the bale aside, reaching up to receive her.

'Come on,' he cried.

Alex took a deep breath and launched herself forward, landing in a pair of powerful hands.

But they were Rinaldo's.

Somehow he had taken Gino's place and was now holding her with his hands about her bare midriff, looking up at her with a face full of grim irony.

'Oi!' Gino protested. 'No need to shove me out of the way like that.'

'There was every need,' Rinaldo said. 'We haven't got time for you two to fool around. This is a busy, working farm.'

'But you had no right—'

'Could you two have your private argument some other time?' Alex demanded, incensed. 'I'd like to get down.'

Rinaldo lowered her to the floor. After her exertions she was breathing hard and heat seemed to be pounding through her body.

'Thank you,' she gasped.

'Do you intend to indulge in these antics very often?' he asked politely.

'I exercise every day. It keeps me fit.'

'Working on the farm has the same effect,' he observed drily. 'You might find it interesting. In the meantime, if you intend to go on doing this, may I suggest you dress more modestly? I don't want my workers distracted.'

He walked away without looking back, so he didn't see Alex lunge after him, only restrained by Gino.

'Save it,' he said.

'I'll kill him!' she muttered. 'I'll kill him!'

'Nah! Fantasise about it like the rest of us do.'

'What does he mean *modestly*?'

'Well, you are quite an eyeful, and an armful.'

He wrapped his arms about her waist, making no effort to release her.

'Well, you'd better let me go,' she said grumpily. 'It wouldn't do for me to *distract* you.'

'You distract me all the time,' he said wistfully.

'Gino!' came a yell from outside.

'Let's kill him together,' Gino muttered, releasing her, resignedly.

Before having breakfast Alex took a cool shower. She felt hot all through, deep down, intensely hot in a way that no water could soothe. The feeling had been there since Rinaldo's hands had encircled her waist, holding her against him.

Perhaps it was lucky, she thought, that Gino had not caught her. He would certainly have turned that intimate moment into a kiss.

But Rinaldo had been completely unmoved.

She rubbed soap over the place, feeling again the pressure of his fingers, and the warmth going through her in endless waves. She turned the water onto cold, and let it lave her again and again, hoping for the feeling to go.

She waited a long time before going downstairs, and when she did she found that the brothers had gone.

Despite the occasional battles Alex found her introduction to Belluna genuinely fascinating. Rinaldo had given her a view from a distance, but now she rode with Gino, getting a closer view of fields full of corn and olives, vineyards stretching away on steep slopes.

'We grow the Sangiovese grapes that make Chianti,' he said. '*True* Chianti, made and bottled in this region. We have our imitators all over the world, but they're not the same.'

His voice contained a hint of Tuscan arrogance, that made Alex smile, realising that there was more to him than an easygoing charmer.

But for pure arrogance, the kind that made her want to dance with rage, she thought there was no beating Rinaldo. He made no comment about their long absences together. The whole matter seemed beneath his notice. Nor did he show much interest when they discussed their adventures in the evening.

He would listen, grunting, to the day's events, then take himself off to his study at the first opportunity.

'He makes me want to bang my head against the wall,' Alex raged one evening when he'd gone.

'Bang *his*,' Gino suggested. 'More fun.'

'Ah, but would I make any impression on it?'

'Not a hope. People have been trying for years.'

'How does anyone put up with him?' Alex asked bitterly. There was something about the way Rinaldo overlooked her that made her seethe.

'It takes long practise,' Gino said, yawning. 'It's been a tiring day.'

'Yes, I'm going straight to bed.'

She had grown even more fond of the bedroom, whose décor and furniture were so far behind the times. She had soon gotten into the Italian habit of stripping off the duvet and all the sheets each morning and hanging them out of the window to air. Teresa protested that a guest should not be working, but Alex enjoyed the job.

She particularly relished the moment when she'd lost her grip, and the duvet fell from the window, landing on

Rinaldo who happened to be underneath. His yell and the infuriated look he cast up at her were among her happiest memories. In fact, much the pleasure of her stay lay in the knowledge that she was infuriating him.

'Teresa is upset with you,' he observed one morning at breakfast.

'Yes, I know. She thinks it's shocking that I do my own room and help her in the kitchen.'

'Then why hurt her feelings?'

'Because I don't want to put any more burdens onto her aching bones. Have either of you any idea how old Teresa is?'

'Older than I can count, I know that,' Gino said.

'Do you really think she can manage this great house with no help?'

'I've offered to get someone else in,' Rinaldo informed her. 'She won't have it.'

Alex made a sound of exasperation intended to cover all men.

'And you left matters there because it was convenient,' she snorted. 'Great!'

'May I remind you that my father was alive until recently?' Rinaldo said coldly. 'It was his decision.'

'Then it was the wrong decision and you should have overruled him. Don't tell me you couldn't have done that. Teresa is an old woman and it's too much for her. She won't admit it because she's proud, and she's afraid you'll send her away.'

'What nonsense! Of course I wouldn't!'

'Don't tell me, tell her. Say she's got to have someone else in to do the heavy work, whether she likes it or not. Be firm. Are you a man or a mouse?'

'I'm beginning to wonder,' he said, eyeing her grimly.

'Oh, stop that! You know I'm right.'

'Heaven preserve me from women who say, "You know I'm right".'

'Yes, because you know they are.'

'Can't you two talk without fighting?' Gino asked plaintively.

Alex shrugged. 'It's as good a way of communicating as any other,' she said, her eyes on Rinaldo. 'At least it's honest. People are never so sincere as when they're abusing each other.'

'I don't understand that,' Gino said.

But Rinaldo understood perfectly. She could see that. He was giving her the same look of ironic complicity that she'd seen after Enrico's funeral. It said that they saw the world through the same eyes, and to hell with the others.

'I'm merely astonished at your extravagance,' he said. 'The more wages I have to pay the longer you have to wait for your money.'

Alex rolled her eyes to heaven.

'Give me patience!' she implored some unseen deity. 'This house is full of empty rooms. The new maid will live in one of them, which will be part of her wages that will cost you nothing. You see? All problems solved.'

'When I consider how anxious I was to bring you here,' Rinaldo observed, 'I can only wonder at my own foolishness.'

'For pity's sake stop arguing,' she told him. 'Just do it. Soften it by telling Teresa she can choose the person herself. She's probably got a relative who'd be ideal. Go on. Do it.'

'You're taking a risk,' Gino muttered, his eyes on his brother as if he was a lion about to spring. 'He doesn't like being ordered about. Never fear. I'll protect you.'

'I can protect myself against Rinaldo perfectly, thank

you,' Alex said, although she too was watching him carefully. 'After all, what can he do to me?'

'Throw you out,' Rinaldo growled.

'Not you,' she jeered. 'You might think you want to, but then you wouldn't have me under your eye. Think of the sleep you'd lose, wondering what I was doing, who I was seeing. No, I'm safe enough.'

'Alex,' Gino begged, 'please be careful.'

'Who wants to be careful? That's boring.' She was enjoying herself.

'I understood,' Rinaldo said frostily, 'that we were to have first refusal.'

'Certainly. That's what I'll tell Montelli and all the others, but who's to say I can't tell them over a candlelit supper?'

'Hey,' Gino said at once, 'if there are any candlelit suppers to be bought, I'll buy them.'

'With champagne?'

'With anything you want, *amor mio*.'

Rinaldo rose sharply and went into the kitchen. A little later they heard the sound of argument and weeping, interspersed with Rinaldo's voice, speaking more gently than Alex had ever heard before.

The next day he drove Teresa to the village where she had been born, about fifty miles away. When they returned in the evening they were accompanied by two hefty young women whom Teresa introduced as her great-nieces, Celia and Franca.

When she had shepherded them into the house Rinaldo detained Alex with a touch on her arm.

'Thank you,' he said gruffly. 'I never thought of it but—you were right.'

Alex smiled. 'She'll be happier with their company, too.'

'I never thought of that either. She and Poppa used to chat in the evenings sometimes, when he wasn't out with Enrico. Since he died she sits in the kitchen alone. Why did you see it and not me?'

'I'm a stranger. Our eyes always see the most clearly.'

'You are no stranger,' he said abruptly, and walked away.

Within a couple of days Celia and Franca had brought the heavy work under their expert control, leaving only the cooking to Teresa. This she guarded jealously.

Whether Rinaldo had told her or whether she had guessed the truth Alex couldn't say. But it was clear that she now regarded Alex as a friend. She would take special care in serving her food, and her eyes would meet hers in a silent question. *Was this how she liked it? Yes? Bene!*

On those occasions Alex would look up to find Rinaldo regarding her, and remember the odd note in his voice when he said, 'You are no stranger.'

She rented another car and, with the knowledge that she now had independence of movement, she no longer felt any need to leave the farm.

Evenings that had once been spent going to parties and first nights were now spent contentedly combing grass seeds out of Brutus's long fur. He came to expect it and would present himself, rolling over on his back to make it easy.

'I used to do that,' Rinaldo observed, 'but these days he tends to stay in the house, so he doesn't wander among the long grass so much, and it stopped being necessary. Until now.'

'He joins me when I run in the morning,' she said. 'At least, he starts out with me, then drops out when he gets tired, and goes and waits for me in the barn. When I swing from the rings he watches in a puzzled sort of way, and you can almost hear him thinking, 'What on earth is she *doing*?'

'We're the best of friends now, aren't we, old boy?' she asked Brutus tenderly. 'And if I don't get these seeds out, you're going to grow a lawn.'

Rinaldo no longer seemed to object to her petting Brutus, and when she looked up a moment later she found him looking at her with a faint smile on his face.

One day he said to her, 'It would be doing me a favour if you'd wait in the house this morning. The vet is coming to give Brutus his injection, and if I'm not back in time at least you'll be with him.'

'Of course. The vet comes all the way out here?'

'You mean, why don't I take Brutus to the surgery? Because he hates cars and goes mad in them, climbing all over the place. That's bad for his arthritis.' After a moment he added uneasily, 'Of course, it costs a lot more—'

'So I'll have to wait an extra five minutes for the money? I wish you'd stop saying things like that.'

'I'm merely trying to assure you that I'm not being wilfully extravagant—'

'No, you're not,' she said indignantly. 'You're rubbing my nose in it. It's worth the expenditure to save Brutus pain, *and you knew I'd say that, so please let it drop.*'

He nodded, and left.

She spent the morning sitting on the sofa with the old dog, who panted in a way she hadn't seen before and was disinclined to move.

At last the vet arrived. He was a youngish man called Silvio, whom Alex liked at once. She explained who she was but had the feeling he already knew. Was there anyone in the whole of Tuscany who didn't know the situation, she wondered?

'How long has he been panting like this?' he asked when he saw Brutus.

'Since this morning. I thought his arthritis must be hurting since it must be so long since his last injection. But the next one will make it all right, won't it?'

'I can take away that pain, but this is something else.' Silvio felt in Brutus's throat, and the dog whined softly. 'There's a lump there, and at his age it's probably bad news. Look at how white his snout is. He's very old. He's had his life. The kindest thing now is to let him go peacefully.'

'I can't authorise you to do that,' Alex said. 'He's Rinaldo's dog.'

'Tell him to call me and I'll come back, preferably today. Rinaldo can't put the inevitable off any longer. Do you still want me to give him the injection?'

'Of course,' she said at once.

When Silvio had gone Alex rubbed the dog's head, laid trustingly in her lap.

'How is he ever going to let you go?' she murmured. 'You were *her* dog. You're all he has of her.'

Gino returned first. When she told him what had happened he dropped to his knees beside Brutus, patting him and murmuring sympathetically.

Rinaldo arrived a few minutes later and Brutus slid off the sofa and went to meet him. He was moving more easily now, and Alex watched the pleasure come into Rinaldo's face as he saw the improvement and ran his hands over the rough coat.

'Thank you,' he told Alex. 'He's still panting a bit though. Did the vet have anything to say about that?'

'Yes, he thinks it's something bad,' Alex said. 'He

wants you to call him and discuss—' she hesitated '—putting him to sleep.'

'Nonsense,' Rinaldo said impatiently. 'A good meal is all he needs.'

'I fed him this afternoon. He only ate a little and then he brought it up.'

'He'll eat what *I* give him. You'll see.'

But Brutus only stared mournfully at the food his master put down for him.

'Come on,' Rinaldo urged gently. 'It's your favourite.'

The dog looked up at him with eyes that Alex couldn't bear to see. They were full of understanding, and trust that his master would face the truth and do what must be done.

Rinaldo saw Alex and Gino looking at him.

'You'd think no dog had ever been off his food before,' he snapped.

He went into the next room and they heard him on the phone to Silvio. When he came back he said,

'He's on his way. I'm going for a walk.'

He didn't speak to Brutus but he looked at him, and the old dog wandered slowly out after his master, into the twilight.

Gino sighed. 'He hasn't seen it yet.'

'He's seen it,' Alex said softly.

Silvio arrived in an hour to find Rinaldo and Brutus sitting under the trees. Gino and Alex went out and arrived as the vet was saying, 'All I can do is give him some tablets, that would keep him with you for a few more weeks. But they wouldn't be happy weeks. Not for him.'

Rinaldo shrugged. 'That settles it. The barn is the best place.'

He began to walk away, Brutus following.

'Shall we come?' Gino asked.

'No need,' Rinaldo said over his shoulder.

Silvio followed them into the barn and remained for ten minutes before coming out and driving away.

After a moment Rinaldo emerged. His manner was calm and his face betrayed nothing. He shut the barn and walked off under the trees.

Alex spent the rest of that evening alone with Gino, talking in a half-hearted fashion.

Rinaldo returned after an hour, brushed aside their attempts at conversation and went straight to his office, where Teresa brought him coffee.

Gino, who made a well-intentioned visit, returned looking glum.

'Rinaldo says he has to concentrate on the books. He says there's work to be done and he can't waste time on something that's finished with. When I left he was studying figures.'

'The ultimate sign of heartlessness, according to him,' Alex said wryly.

'Heartless is right,' Gino snapped.

Rinaldo had not appeared when Alex went to bed. She tried to sleep but couldn't, and at last she got up and went to stand at the window, where a full moon was turning the land to silver.

Suddenly she grew still. From down below she could see movement, as though someone was hiding just beyond the trees.

Pulling on her dressing gown she left her room and went along the corridor to Rinaldo's room. But her knock produced no response. After a moment she knocked louder, but still there was no answer.

She stood in the hallway, listening to the quiet of the

house about her, unwilling to try again and awake Rinaldo for what might be nothing. She could imagine his caustic remarks.

After a moment she turned away and went down the stairs, into the corridor that led to the back door. She could just make out that that there was still someone beyond the trees. Now she could also hear the sound of rhythmic movement.

She stepped forward as silently as possible, gliding through the trees until she came to a small clearing. Then she stopped. What she saw made her draw a sharp breath and step back quickly.

The man in the clearing would not want anyone to see what he was doing, and especially he would not want to be seen by her.

The spade flashed as the hole grew deeper. Rinaldo stood inside, waist deep. He wore no shirt and his body gleamed with perspiration as it rose and fell. His concentration was fierce and total.

At last he stopped, leaning on the spade, his head bent, his shoulders heaving. Then he straightened up, and reached out to something Alex had not noticed before.

Now she saw that Brutus was lying on the ground. She waited for Rinaldo to toss him into the grave, but instead he drew the cold body toward him and gathered it into his arms. Slowly he began to lower it.

Alex held her breath, awed by his incredible gentleness to an animal who could no longer feel it.

At the last moment he paused and laid his cheek against Brutus's head. For a long time he was still. Then he moved his head slightly, caressing the fur, and she thought she saw something shining on his cheek. Still he held his friend, as though unable to face the final moment.

'*Perdona mi! Ti prego perdona mi!*'

Forgive me. Please forgive me. The last words she had ever expected to hear from this unrelenting man.

At last he dropped to his knees, out of Alex's sight. He remained there for a long time.

She backed away slowly, knowing that he must not find her here. When she was safely out of the trees she began to run back to the house. As she went, she called herself a fool.

She had never known anything about Rinaldo. Or rather, she had known exactly what he wanted her to know, and no more. Tonight she had witnessed a consuming grief that he would keep hidden from the world, if he could.

Nobody saw her slip into the house, for which she was thankful. She wouldn't have known what to say to Gino just now.

Once in her room she went to the window and waited. At last, after a long time, he emerged from the trees. She stepped back from the window, lest he see her, but he walked with his head down and his shoulders hunched, not looking about him. As she watched, he crossed the yard and disappeared.

At breakfast next morning Rinaldo looked as though he hadn't slept. Which was probably true, Alex thought. His face was pale beneath his tan, and she could see the tension about his mouth

She longed to say something that would ease his pain, but she knew he would never let her get so close, and would resent her for even trying.

He didn't sit down, but snatched up a coffee in one hand and a roll in the other, eating on his feet as though longing to be gone.

Gino came into the kitchen, looking worried.

'I've just been to the barn. Brutus has gone.'

Rinaldo shrugged. 'So?'

'I thought we might bury him properly.'

'What for?' Rinaldo asked coldly.

'What for? You loved him. I did too, but you and he were so close—'

'He was a dog, Gino. Dogs come and go.'

'But—'

'I've already disposed of him.'

'*Disposed* of him?' Gino echoed, aghast. 'Like a piece of rubbish? That was Brutus! How can you be so callous?'

'He was dead,' Rinaldo said, his voice on the edge of exasperation. 'There was nothing more to say or do. He was dead.'

'So you just threw him out. No grave, no—'

'I advise you to grow up and stop being sentimental,' Rinaldo said coldly.

He drained his cup and walked out quickly before his brother could speak again.

'Well, I'll be—!' Gino almost tore his hair. 'He was supposed to love that dog. Some kind of love!'

'People have their own way of showing their feelings,' Alex suggested.

'Always supposing that they have any feelings. Brutus is dead. Chuck him out! That's how Rinaldo sees it. He didn't even cry when the poor old fellow died.'

'You don't know. We weren't there.'

'You saw his face when he came out of the barn. Blank.'

'But that doesn't mean anything,' Alex protested, thinking about the tell-tale gleam she'd seen the night before, as Rinaldo laid his face against the lifeless dog.

'He wouldn't let anyone see. He'd probably think it was weakness.'

'Rinaldo thinks *having* feelings is weakness, never mind showing them. That's why he cuts them right out.'

For the first time she found herself irritated by Gino.

'I'll bet you don't know half as much as you think you do,' she said. 'Maybe a stranger can pick up more—'

'Oh ho! Here comes woman's intuition!'

'Here comes the coffee to pour over your head if you talk like that.'

He grinned and hopped nimbly out of the way.

'Pax! I take it back. But trust me on this. I understand Rinaldo as you never will.'

And I, she thought, am beginning to understand him in way that nobody else does.

She didn't know what else to say. She longed to make Gino see the truth about his brother, but it was Rinaldo's secret and she had no right to betray it.

CHAPTER SEVEN

FRUSTRATED, she went out into the yard. A movement from the barn drew her steps there, and she found Rinaldo.

'Have you come to tell me what a heartless monster I am, too?' he asked ironically. 'Because if so, don't.'

'No, I won't say that. After last night, I know better.'

He shot her a sharp glance. 'What do you mean?'

'I saw you bury Brutus.'

For a moment he was quite still. Then he said curtly, 'Nonsense.'

'It isn't. I noticed something moving in the trees and went down. I was there while you dug the grave and put him in it. I saw—everything.'

'You have a vivid imagination, I'll say that for you. You and Gino make a good pair.'

Anger at his rebuff made her snap, 'You think Gino would be interested in what I saw? Let's try.'

She turned to go but he was beside her in a flash, seizing her arms in a fierce grip.

'Don't dare to tell him anything,' he growled. 'What concern is it of yours what I do?'

'But it's true, isn't it? Losing him broke your heart. Why deny it?'

'Because it's nobody else's business!'

'But he's your brother. Don't you think he'd feel for you?'

'I don't ask him to feel for me. Nor do I ask you.'

'Who do you ask?' she said quietly. 'Now Brutus is dead, who do you share your feelings with?'

'There's a lot to be said for a dog,' he snapped. 'They keep quiet and they don't fret about things that are none of their business. Why did you have to come Belluna and interfere?'

'You more or less forced me to come.'

'And it was the worst day's work I ever did.'

'You said I needed to learn about this place and the things that went on in it. That's just what I'm doing. I'm learning that nothing is ever quite what it seems.'

'What does that mean?'

'You, for instance. You work hard at being one thing and seeming another. I wonder why.'

'It keeps me safe from snoopers.'

'Does that include Gino? Because you hide from him too. You don't let anyone in, do you? Except Brutus.'

His fingers tightened on her shoulders, giving her a tiny shake.

'Will you stop?' he asked fiercely. *'Will you stop?'*

'I'm sorry,' she said gently after a moment. 'I know it isn't really my business. But now I can't help getting involved. Where do I draw the line?'

'Right here,' he said, still holding her. 'You've reached the boundary. Stay on your side of it, and we'll manage.'

Suddenly she realised that he was shaking. Through the contact of his fingers on her bare arms she could sense his whole body vibrating.

In her turn she reached up to take hold of his arms.

'Rinaldo,' she said. 'Don't shut me out. Let me help.'

'I don't need your help.'

But she refused to be snubbed. 'After last night it's too late,' she said quietly. 'I know what I know.'

She knew she was treading on dangerous ground and

for a moment she thought he would lose his temper. But instead he sighed and the anger went out of his face.

'How can *you* possibly help?' he asked heavily.

'You mean I'm the last person who ever could. Because I caused all the trouble, didn't I?'

Hearing his own accusation put so bluntly seemed to do something to Rinaldo. She saw his eyes full of shock as he realised that he was still holding her. He dropped his hands from her arms.

There was an ache inside her that had something to do with his misery. She wanted to assuage it and ease the hurt for them both.

He sat down on a bale of hay, leaning back against a post of the barn, his hands hanging loose as though he'd lost the will to fight.

'No, it's not your fault,' he said tiredly. 'I know I said that at first, but in truth I know better. It wasn't you who created the situation.'

He took a long breath. His face was livid.

'It was my father,' he said at last. 'A man I trusted, and who let me live in a fool's paradise. He never warned me, that's what—' He made a confused gesture.

'That's what hurts, isn't it?' she whispered, sitting beside him.

His eyes were full of resignation, almost despair.

'Yes,' he said simply. 'We used to sit up late at night, discussing problems. I thought we were a team, and all the time he was keeping me at a distance, not trusting me with the truth.'

'Oh, no,' she said at once. 'It wasn't like that.'

'How can you possibly know?'

'Because in an odd way I feel as if I do know him. Everyone talks about how lovely he was, laughing, singing, always looking on the bright side. I think that prob-

An Important Message from the Editors

Dear Reader,

Because you've chosen to read one of our fine romance novels, we'd like to say "thank you!" And, as a special way to thank you, we've selected two more of the books you love so well, plus an exciting Mystery Gift, to send you absolutely FREE!

Please enjoy them with our compliments...

Pam Powers

Peel off Seal and Place Inside...

EDITOR'S
FREE GIFT
SEAL
THANK YOU

How to validate your Editor's
FREE GIFT
"Thank You"

1. Peel off gift seal from front cover. Place it in space provided at right. This automatically entitles you to receive 2 FREE BOOKS and a fabulous mystery gift.

2. Send back this card and you'll get 2 brand-new Harlequin Romance® novels. These books have a cover price of $3.99 each in the U.S. and $4.50 each in Canada, but they are yours to keep absolutely free.

3. There's no catch. You're under no obligation to buy anything. We charge nothing—ZERO—for your first shipment. And you don't have to make any minimum number of purchases—not even one!

4. The fact is, thousands of readers enjoy receiving their books by mail from the Harlequin Reader Service®. They enjoy the convenience of home delivery...they like getting the best new novels at discount prices BEFORE they're available in stores...and they love their *Heart to Heart* subscriber newsletter featuring author news, horoscopes, recipes, book reviews and much more!

5. We hope that after receiving your free books you'll want to remain a subscriber. But the choice is yours—to continue or cancel, any time at all! So why not take us up on our invitation, with no risk of any kind. You'll be glad you did!

6. Remember...just for validating your Editor's Free Gift Offer, we'll send you THREE gifts, *ABSOLUTELY FREE!*

GET A *Free* MYSTERY GIFT...

SURPRISE MYSTERY GIFT COULD BE YOURS _FREE_ AS A SPECIAL "THANK YOU" FROM THE EDITORS OF HARLEQUIN

Visit us online at
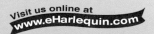
www.eHarlequin.com